HORSE OF A DIFFERENT COLOR

HORSE OF A DIFFERENT COLOR

A MECANA NOVEL BY

JOHN L. LANSDALE

BOOKVOICE PUBLISHING 2018

This novel is a work of fiction. All incidents and all characters are fictionalized, with the exception that well-known historical and public figures are products of the author's imagination and are not to be construed as real. Where real-life historical figures appear, the situations and dialogues concerning those persons are fictional and are not intended to depict actual events within the fictional confines of the story. In all other respects, any resemblance to persons living or dead is entirely coincidental.

ISBN
978-1-949381-07-8 Paperback
978-0-9990361-4-3 Hardcover
978-0-9990361-3-6 eBook

BookVoice Publishing
PO Box 1528
Chandler, TX 75758
www.bookvoicepublishing.com

THE MECANA SERIES by John L. Lansdale
#1 - Horse of a Different Color
#2 - When the Night Bird Sings
#3 - Twisted Justice

Titles by John L. Lansdale
Slow Bullet
Zombie Gold
The Last Good Day
Broken Moon
Shadows West (with Joe R. Lansdale)
Hell's Bounty (with Joe R. Lansdale)
Boy and Hog (Short Story)
Emergency Christmas (Short Story)
Tales from the Crypt (Comic Series)
That Hellbound Train (Graphic Novel)
Yours Truly, Jack the Ripper (Graphic Novel)
Shadow Warrior (Graphic Novel)
Justin Case (Graphic Novel)

Follow the author online at
www.bookvoicepublishing.com
www.twitter.com/mybookvoice
www.goodreads.com/johnllansdale
www.facebook.com/bookvoicepublishing

<u>What Others are Saying about John L. Lansdale</u>

"Mickey Spillane fans will welcome this page-turner... Lansdale effectively delays revealing the novel's big secret until the end. Those who like their thrillers with a heavy dose of violent action will be satisfied."
– *Publishers Weekly* review of **Slow Bullet**

"This is an entertaining, science fiction-historical-horror blend with resourceful protagonists and a solid cast of secondary characters." – *Booklist* review of **Zombie Gold**

"...the author's innate ability to spin a complex tale painted with vivid characters and intense suspense provides readers with a well-paced book that they may find difficult to set down...a worthwhile suspenseful ride."
– *Amazing Stories* review of **Horse of a Different Color**

"**Slow Bullet** is a straight-ahead thriller...it's about action, and there's plenty of that. Check it out."
– *Bill Crider's Pop Culture Magazine*

"**Zombie Gold** has something for everyone... It's exciting, entertaining and educational. A fun ride."
– Joan Hallmark, TV personality, actress and author

"...something unique and comfortable and difficult to put down. Highly recommended."
– *Cemetery Dance* review of **Hell's Bounty**

"True to Lansdale tradition, John L. Lansdale has compiled a piece of work that should appeal to a wide range of readers." – *Amazing Stories* review of **Zombie Gold**

For Pam,
A real detective.

"Who knows what evil lurks in the hearts of men."
The Shadow radio drama

PROLOGUE

Officer Down

Fifth Ward Projects
Houston, Texas
12:05 A.M.

She lay on the bare mattress, naked, in a spread-eagle position on her back; her beautiful body drenched in sweat and her wet green eyes wide with fear. Her mouth was covered with duct tape and her hands and feet bound to the bed post with leather straps. A foul smell of dampness and decay filled the empty room.

Rain drops tapped on the dirty windows and the car lights made the rain drops look like sparkling rhinestones as they slid down the windows in the wee hours of the night.

A door opened and a tall, wet shadow appeared in the open doorway. She could make out the vague image of a gun. Tears ran down her cheeks; she fought at the straps.

She screamed but no sound came out. The shadow stepped inside the door and shined a flashlight on her.

"It's alright, I'm a cop," he said.

She closed her eyes and sighed. They found her. She had been rescued. Her prayers were answered.

Suddenly, a second shadow appeared in the doorway behind the first, holding something long and shiny. She squirmed and darted her eyes back and forth, shook her head up and down as a warning, but the dark night betrayed her and the cop kept moving toward her.

Then she saw it. It was a knife, a killing knife, in the hand of the dark figure behind the cop. In the blink of an eye, the knife plunged into his body. Blood gushed out and ran down his back. He crumbled to the floor, his gun sliding from his hand.

Houston Memorial Hospital
One Month Later

In Room 649 of the physical rehabilitation ward, Rustin Kemp struggled to raise his thirty-year-old, six-foot-three body up in bed on the pull-up bar. His blue eyes showed the pain as he tugged on the bar.

Sunlight splashed across the walls of the room through a window on a bright autumn day, painting them with a multi-colored pattern. A red porcelain vase with a dozen red roses in it and a card propped against it read, "Get well soon - from all the gang."

Rustin's boss, Captain Bill Lucas, stood beside the bed, his thin brown hair showing a shiny bald spot. Sagging jaws rested on the collar of a white shirt under a dark blue suit coat and a red tie draped over a pudgy belly swung back and forth like a pendulum.

"Everyone wanted to let you know they were thinking of you," he said. "Thought I would deliver the flowers and see how you were doing. The son of a bitch left you for dead."

Rustin dropped his hands from the pull bar, adjusted his pillow and looked at Bill Lucas.

"Can't walk yet," he said, "but the Doc thinks I will. I won't be doing any dancing, but I may be able to get around good enough to find that bastard if it's the last thing I ever do."

"I hope so, Rustin, but as my daddy used to say on the farm, 'We got a hard row to hoe.' No DNA, nothing except the horrific things he did to her. Homicide has had a crew on the case ever since you went down. It looks like she partied too hard and ran into the wrong guy. He may be in jail for something else, or laying low for a while."

"He'll show up," Rustin said. "The sick ones always do. I have to get out of this bed. There's something in the back of my mind that keeps bugging me. Something I need to re-member that won't come to me."

"Rustin, if you hadn't been chasing that crackhead and stumbled in on her she may have disappeared like a lot of the others, and then no one would have known what hap-pened to her. Unfortunately, it didn't turn out good. But at least her family got to bury her."

"All the more reason I have to find him, Bill."

"What you need to do is concentrate on getting well."

"I am, and I'll be planning how I'm going to catch that son of a bitch, too."

"You're a hard-headed man, Rustin."

"Been told that before."

Bill laughed and patted Rustin on the arm.

"Oh, I'm going to walk again. You can count on that."

"If you need anything let me know."

"I will. Tell everyone at the station I said thanks."

PART ONE

1

One Year Later

Julie Crawford just turned twenty-one. She was celebrating her adulthood on a Saturday night in downtown Warfield, Texas with friends and some of the club regulars at Griffin's Bar and Grill. Griffin's looked like a bastard cousin to Applebee's, with a smaller menu and a longer bar.

"Hey everybody," Julie said, standing up. "This is my last night at Griffin's. My grandpa left me a bundle; I'm headed to Hollywood to be an actress! I don't have to worry about going to law school anymore to please mommy and daddy."

A tall, thin, elderly gentleman in the back of the room with white hair to his shoulders stood up holding a glass of beer. "I propose a toast to the birthday girl," he said. "She's certainly pretty enough to be a movie star. I'm old enough to remember June Allison. Julie reminds me of her, and the world could use another June Allison."

Everyone stood up, raised their glasses, gave a cheer and drank.

"Thanks everybody!" Julie said. "That's Mr. Rod Burger, my private drama coach who proposed the toast. He's a little prejudiced since my folks pay him a small fortune to train me."

Everyone laughed.

About midnight, Julie went to pee and never came back.

Two days later, two guys fishing found her mutilated body floating in the Trinity River. The police report said it would be a week before the cause of death could be determined.

At the request of the Warfield Police Department, Dallas PD sent fifteen-year veteran Detective Thomas Mecana to investigate.

Mecana was a tall, square-jawed, good-looking poster-type ex-Marine with brown wavy hair and penetrating gray eyes. He prided himself on staying fit and looked ten years younger than his forty-two-year-old body: A complete opposite to the Police Chief of Warfield, who looked like an eggplant.

Mecana's wife divorced him and moved to Austin ten years ago with his two daughters. For caring more about his job than his family, she claimed.

After researching a variety of recent murders, Mecana discovered that a murder in Houston had something in common with Julie. The vagina had been removed from both victims. Could be this sicko had come to Warfield, Mecana thought, and there would be more murders. Most of the information Mecana passed on to the Warfield Police was wasted. They wanted it all to go away and to get back to writing speeding tickets and working security for private businesses for extra money.

Warfield Police Chief David Orr was working on his second McDonalds Super Breakfast when the telephone rang.

"Warfield Police, Chief Orr speaking."

"Chief, my name's Rustin Kemp. I was involved in the Belmont murder case here in Houston last year. The Crawford murder sounds like the same MO."

"Yeah, you're not the only one. We got a detective here on the Crawford case that thinks it might be the same guy. I remember reading about you last year," Orr said. "He stabbed you and got away." Orr stuck a fork in a piece of sausage and jammed it in his mouth. "You still on the Houston force?"

"Doing private eye work now. I want that son of a bitch bad. I wanted to come up and take a look."

"Don't have a problem with that. I'll take all the help I can get, but you'll have to clear it with Detective Tom Mecana in Dallas. He's the lead guy on the case."

"I've heard of him. I'll call him, Chief. Thanks."

"No problem," Orr said, and went back to eating his breakfast.

2

Rustin looked up from his pancakes and saw Bill Lucas coming toward him. He wondered why Bill was at IHOP, he usually ate breakfast at home. He would always say, with a laugh, that nobody could cook instant oatmeal better than his Amy.

"Thought I would find you here," Bill said.

Rustin removed his cane from the empty chair and offered Bill a seat.

"Man, looking at those pancakes makes me hungry," Lucas said.

"I thought Amy always fixed your breakfast."

"I cheat sometimes," Bill said and sat down.

A cute, dark-haired waitress with 'Maria' on her name tag stopped at the table, poured Bill a cup of coffee and asked if he was ready to order.

"Yes. I'll have a stack of blueberry pancakes and sausage to go with my coffee, Maria."

"That oatmeal didn't go very far, huh, Bill?"

"Don't tell Amy. She's always nagging me about my weight."

"Not a word, I promise," Rustin said, grinning.

"Good. Got a call from Tom Mecana yesterday," Lucas said and took a sip of coffee. "You know who he is?"

"Yes. He's probably solved more murder cases than anyone else in Texas."

"Right. He wanted to know why you were trying to butt in on his case. I told him you didn't work for me anymore and I didn't have a clue what he was talking about. He said he didn't need any half-ass cops. I got to thinking about it this morning, figured you would be here since Debbie decided to take a powder, and find out what the hell was going on."

"I haven't talked to him," Rustin said. "The Police Chief in Warfield must have. The case he's talking about is a lot like the Belmont one. I was going to have a look but I needed his approval. I guess that's a no."

"Get you a client. Maybe the girl's folks. He may not help you but he can't stop you from earning a living."

"True. That would give me the right to be there," Rustin said, and took the last bite of his pancakes and reached for his wallet.

The waitress brought Bill his breakfast and poured him a fresh cup of coffee. He wolfed the pancakes down, pushed the empty plate away and picked up his coffee cup.

"Heard anything from Debbie?" he asked, and blew on the coffee.

"Nope, she said she needed to get away for a while to think things over. That was last Friday, haven't heard a word from her since. Her sister called for her, said she was at her folks'. Knew I would be worried. What she couldn't handle was me being a cripple."

"Well if that's her reason you're probably better off with out her. Think she would have done the same thing if you had been wounded in Iraq?"

"Don't know. Got out of there without a scratch and then this happens. You never know what cards you're going to be dealt."

"Good thing you don't have any kids to worry about."

"We tried. After three miscarriages we gave up."

"You should have called for backup that night. Maybe things would be different. You wouldn't be in this shape."

"Like they say, hindsight is 20/20. I thought I could handle it."

"Sounds like he's back in business," Bill said, holding his empty cup up for Maria to see.

"Don't know for sure what I'm going to do. Everything seems to get more complicated every day."

"Only you can decide that, partner. But it should be over for you. Let it go before you wind up getting hurt, physically and mentally."

"I know you mean well, Bill, but it's easier said than done. It won't let me go. It's chewing my insides up." The waitress passed by with the coffee pot, looked at Bill and poured him another cup. "I'll let you know what I decide to do, Bill, thanks."

Rustin picked up his cane and stood up. "My treat," he said, and dropped a twenty on the table.

"Thanks. Take care," Lucas said.

Rustin nodded and limped away.

3

Rustin arrived at the rehab center ten minutes before his appointment, took a couple of pain pills and made a call to Debbie's parents in Beaumont. They said she was there but didn't want to talk to him. She was going to file for divorce and her lawyer would be in touch. That was that.

The therapy lasted an extra hour because the doctor said he was not making enough progress with his weight lifts. He needed to strengthen his leg muscles more to compensate for the nerve damage in his back. Debbie would have agreed with that. When they had sex she had to do all the work. That wouldn't be a problem anymore.

Eight years down the drain. He thought about driving to Beaumont and begging her to come back, but it would probably be a waste of time and he wasn't sure his pride would let him do it any way.

He did ten more lifts with the leg weights, pulled himself up to a sitting position, picked up his cane, placed both hands on it and lifted himself up, leaning on the cane. The right leg was the one he supported most of his weight on, and the left with the cane. The pain got really bad sometimes; he needed his pills to keep going.

His doctor quit writing prescriptions for fear of him becoming addicted and told him to get some over-the-counter pain medicine if he needed it. That was a moot point now. With a new doctor in Dallas he should be able to get what he needed, at least for a while.

He reached in his pocket, got his phone and dialed.

He heard a voice say, "Lucas here."

"Bill, I decided to go to Dallas to find that prick. I wanted to say goodbye and thank you for everything."

"I understand where you're coming from, son, but don't you think you should quit while you're ahead and just move on? You're working with a big disadvantage."

"That has occurred to me but I don't have much of a life at the moment anyway, and those young women he mutilated never had a chance at any kind of life. A leopard can't change his spots. It has to be him. He leaves a gruesome calling card."

"That he does. Keep in touch."

"I will. See you."

Rustin limped to his Ford Explorer and drove home to an empty house. Everywhere he looked he saw reminders of Debbie. She was his high school sweetheart. He was the quarterback and she was a pretty blonde-haired, blue-eyed cheerleader. They had big dreams for their future. Everyone said they looked like the perfect couple.

He dropped his cane to the floor, sat down on the bed and tears came rolling down his cheeks. The only reason he had for living was to catch that bastard.

He wiped the tears away, packed a suitcase and decided he would wait until he got to Dallas to call his mom and dad to watch the house. He locked the front door, put the key in the mailbox, put his suitcase in the Explorer and headed up Interstate 45 to Dallas, into a setting sun and the unknown.

4

Mecana ordered a beer and looked up at the TV. Monday night football was on, something he never got into much. Griffin's was full of twenty-something college students. Some faculty members came in and he hoped he would blend in with them.

He noticed a pretty redhead wearing a revealing red dress at the end of the bar; four empty margarita glasses in front of her.

She raised a fifth salted glass to her crimson red lips, finished it off, got up and tilted to the left as she moved down the bar to where Mecana was sitting. She pushed a stool in between him and a little, skinny nerd-looking-guy. The nerd gave her a dirty look but said nothing, only slid off his stool, picked up his beer and walked away.

"Hi," she said. "Buy a lady a drink?"

At closer range Mecana could see her long red hair, cream-smooth skin and sparkling blue eyes, the cleavage of perfectly sculptured breasts and her long strong legs as she climbed up on the bar stool next to him.

"Don't you think you've had enough?" he said.

"Goodness no, I'm just getting started. My boyfriend dumped me, thought I would get drunk. You want to help me?"

"You must have a dumb boyfriend."

"You a teacher?" she asked.

"No. I stopped in to watch the game."

"You want to take me home, get in my pants?"

"You're drunk."

"I sure am. My name's Kinky, what's yours?"

"Mine's Tom. Kinky's an odd name for such a pretty girl."

"Got another one I don't like. You do want to get in my pants don't cha? Been watching you, you're a good-looking dude. You got a wife?"

"No."

"Don't matter; I fuck for the fun of it anyway."

"I think you need to call it a night, young lady. You got a friend here that could drive you home?"

"Nope. I don't know what happened to my ride. You're it."

"I'll call you a taxi, my treat. Go home and sleep it off. The world will look better tomorrow."

"Buy me another round and I'll consider it," she said and smiled, showing her perfect white teeth.

Mecana thought about his teenage daughters, and the perils of growing up. "Alright, I'll buy you one more and you go home. Deal?"

"You sure you don't want to go with me?"

"I'm sure. Margarita, right?"

"Right. I like big ones with lots of salt," she stuck her finger in her mouth, rolled it around and sucked on it.

Mecana shook his head, waved at the bartender.

A little guy with short black hair, a goatee and both arms full of tattoos walked over and leaned on the edge of the bar. He pointed to Mecana's beer bottle. "Another beer, mister?"

"Give me another beer and a large margarita for the lady."

The bartender looked at Kinky, then back to Mecana. "Don't you think you're a little old for her?"

"Just bring me the drinks," Mecana said, and dropped a twenty on the bar. "Keep the change." There was a roar from the crowd. Somebody scored a touchdown.

The bartender gave him a hard look, picked up the twenty and moved away.

Kinky looked at Mecana and laughed. "I think you're just right, Tom," she said. He couldn't help but chuckle too.

"We made a deal, Kinky. After you drink this one I'll call a taxi to take you home."

"I'd like it better if you came with me."

"I don't think so." Mecana was spending too much time with Kinky. He didn't have time to observe the clientele for anything unusual. He had good instincts for that sort of thing. That's why he came, but it wouldn't be tonight.

Kinky devoured the margarita in a few gulps and Mecana called a taxi. He walked her outside. She got in the cab with his help and mumbled her address to the driver. Mecana gave the driver thirty bucks and asked if that would cover it. The driver nodded yes. He closed the door and the cab pulled away.

He felt good about sending her home. By tomorrow she would be sober. The boyfriend a small bump in the road as she got on with her life.

He thought about his daughters again and how much he missed them, got in his Silverado and headed home. He didn't feel like playing cops and robbers anymore tonight.

5

Rustin woke up the next morning a little after eight in Warfield in Room 38 at the Sunset Inn in a king size bed. That was about the only thing the place had going for it. A look at all the ten-year-old cars parked at the orange motel doors were a reminder of his financial status. A policeman's pension was just above the poverty level, and his savings had already run out.

A more immediate problem was obtaining pills. He would have to find a doctor that didn't question him too much or insist that he provide his medical records before writing a prescription.

He stopped for some coffee at McDonalds, and went in search of a doctor. There were only four listed in Warfield.

The one that ran a 'Doc in the Box' emergency clinic in a small strip center looked the best. The cane helped.

He picked up his prescription at Walgreens and headed for the Warfield police station.

The police station was a wooden building, about the size of a three car garage, painted a sea green with white trim. A police cruiser was parked out front. City Hall was across the street in a small red brick building. The mayor and four councilmen all had reserved parking spaces in front. If you didn't see the 'Population: 832' sign coming into town you wouldn't even know you had left Dallas.

Rustin opened the door of the Explorer and stepped out, made his way to the station door and went in. An obese man in his fifties wearing a police uniform was sitting at a desk at the back of the one-room building, chomping on a Big Mac. A sign on the desk said 'Chief David Orr.'

He had a bad haircut, bushy eyebrows, droopy brown eyes and fat jaws. He saw Rustin, swallowed hard and took a drink of Coke. "What can I do for you, sir?" he asked.

"Chief, my name's Rustin Kemp. I spoke with you the other day about the Julie Crawford case. My former boss said Tom Mecana called him and was less than enthusiastic about me coming."

"Yes," Orr said. "I talked to him about it. He said you'd be in the way and might get yourself hurt again and he didn't want that responsibility. I can't go against him."

"I can understand that but I'm here until this nut is caught by Mecana, me or whoever." "Don't expect any help from me. You get out of line, I'll have you arrested."

The door opened and Mecana walked in wearing a blue shirt, a half-zipped gray windbreaker, jeans and black loafers.

"There's the man now. Talk to him," Orr said and picked up his Coke.

"Talk to me about what?" Mecana asked, looking at Rustin.

"About the Crawford case," Rustin said. "I'm Rustin Kemp. I came here to find a killer."

"Oh yeah. The guy who fucked up; let the asshole get away when he murdered the Belmont girl. Best you stay out of my way. You don't, I'll put your ass in jail. "

"There are a lot of threats being thrown around," Rustin said. "I may have made some mistakes but I'm not giving up. Somebody has to catch him."

"I'll get him. You wouldn't be much help anyway, walking on a cane. Go back to Houston. When I catch him I'll let you know. You can come up for the trial, if I don't have to kill him."

"I heard you've been known to crack a few heads," Rustin said.

"When needed. That's why I'm still alive. You hesitate and they bury you," Mecana said.

"That's the damn truth," Orr said, looking at Rustin. "That's why you're in the shape you're in, boy."

"That's your opinion, not the board's," Rustin said.

"I know about that too," Mecana said. "The board cleared you but I don't think I want you watching my back."

"Me neither," Orr added.

"I know you're one of the best, Mecana," Rustin said. "I was hoping we could work together. If we can't, so be it. Sorry you feel that way. I have to do this. I'm at the Sunset Inn for now, if you want to talk."

"Don't sit by the phone, Kemp."

"See you around," Rustin said and limped toward the front door.

6

Chief Orr was munching on a chocolate donut when the phone rang. He answered with a full mouth and somehow managed to get, "Warfield Police," out without choking.

"This is Detective Winslow from the Dallas Homicide Department. Is Tom Mecana there?"

"No, but I'm expecting him any minute."

"I tried to get him at his number, but no answer. There's been another murder he needs to know about. She lived in your town. That's two. You got a real monster on your hands, Chief. They fished her out of the Trinity this morning. Have him call me at the number on your ID when he comes in. He can fill you in, after I talk to him."

"Sure," Orr said, eyeing the donut. When Mecana didn't show up by noon, and Orr couldn't get him on the phone, he sent a car to his address. He wasn't there.

At 5PM, Mecana was still missing and no one had seen him.

About 7:30 that evening there was a knock on Rustin's motel room door. There stood the last person he was expecting - Mecana.

"This is a surprise," Rustin said. "What changed your mind?"

Mecana stepped inside and plopped down on the corner of the bed like his legs wouldn't hold him up anymore. He looked at Rustin and wiped his red eyes. "The murderer has struck again, and I think I helped him."

"What do you mean you helped him?"

"I went to Griffin's bar night before last to check it out. I meet a young lady there who was very drunk. I sent her home in a taxi, alone. They found her mutilated body this morning. I heard it on the scanner on the way to work. At first it didn't register. They said her name was Barbara Jean Sadler. I took off for the crime scene. When I got there, I took a look at the body. It was the girl I put in the taxi. The examiner said she had been dead approximately twenty-four hours. That would have been the night I sent her home alone. She called herself Kinky. Should have drove her home. Been riding around all day trying to decide what to do, thought about you. Know how you feel now. What's going on in your head? I made a mistake and it cost another human being her life. I wanted to come by and apologize for the things I said to you."

"No need to apologize but I'm glad you understand. A young woman died when I fucked up too lost my wife, my job and my self-respect. I'll never be the man I was again. We both made mistakes, bad ones, and we can't undo them. I've spent the last year thinking about it. The only thing we can do is catch this monster and stop the killings. If you want to give up that's your business, but I could use your expertise. I'm not a homicide detective, but either way I'm going to find him."

Mecana dropped his head and sighed. "You're right, Kemp. I owe it to Kinky to find her murderer."

"If you mean that, Mecana, I think we can solve this case. There has to be something we haven't looked at hard enough or long enough."

"There always is," Mecana said, and sat back down on the bed. "I'll check the forensic info and the autopsy reports on Kinky and the Crawford girl, see if I can speed it up. Kinky said she broke up with her boy friend. It might be interesting to see what he has to say. It shouldn't be too hard to find him."

Rustin nodded in agreement.

7

It was 5:30 in the afternoon the next day when Rustin Kemp and Tom Mecana found the address they were looking for. The bartender at Griffin's gave them a name and a police rap sheet gave them the address, 2410 East Fairmont. The old houses on the street had seen better days.

Two teenage boys wearing ass-hugger pants, cowboy caps turned backwards and fancy-looking Nike shoes quickly walked away. The Explorer had a plain-Jane honky look with two white dudes in it. It was like 'COPS' was written all over it. Mecana spotted the number they were looking for and motioned to Rustin to pull over. He parked and they got out.

Rustin managed to make it up the two rickety steps to the front door, and Mecana went around to the back. Rustin moved to one side of the door and knocked on it. No answer. He glanced at the big Harley Davidson sitting in the driveway. Someone was home. Nobody would leave a Harley unattended in this neighborhood.

About the time Rustin started to knock on the door again, it flew open and a young, tall, thin black man, with bushy hair and wearing jeans and a t-shirt, ran by him and headed for the Harley.

Mecana came charging around the corner from the back of the house and tackled him. He fell onto the side of the Harley and knocked it over. Mecana jumped up, drew his gun and yelled at the young man. "Police! Stay on the ground and put your hands on your head!"

"Shit!" the young man exclaimed, and stretched his arms up on his head.

Rustin made his way down the steps and walked up beside Mecana, who still had his Glock pointed at the man on the ground. "Your name DeMax Baker?" Rustin asked.

"Yeah," he said, eyeing Rustin.

"Street name 'Stitch?'"

"Some folks call me that."

"You got some ID?"

"My back pocket."

Rustin leaned on his cane, reached down and removed DeMax's wallet and looked at his drivers license, then dropped the wallet on the ground beside him. "Okay, why you running, DeMax?"

"Didn't know you were cops. Thought you were some of them drug dealers, come to rob me."

"You got some stuff they want, DeMax?" Mecana asked.

"Ain't no dealer."

"You don't sound too convincing."

"Got nothing else to say. Can I get up?"

Mecana holstered his Glock, pulled handcuffs off his belt, stuck the wallet back in DeMax's pants, clamped the handcuffs on his wrist and lifted him to his feet.

A chubby-faced black woman in an old white Ford Taurus stopped in the middle of the street and stuck her head out the window, watching.

DeMax looked Rustin over. "Didn't know cripples could be cops."

"Shut up," Mecana said.

"You know a Barbara Sadler, DeMax?" Rustin asked.

"Might," he said.

"Did you know she's dead?"

"Yeah, saw it on TV this mornin'."

"The bartender at Griffin's said you were Kinky's boyfriend. You don't seem very broken up over the fact she's dead," Rustin said.

"Ain't nothin' I can do for you cops to find the mudderfucker who did it. Me and Kinky hooked up a few times, don't know if you could say we boyfriend-girlfriend."

"She seemed to think so. Said you broke up. Why?" Mecana said.

DeMax twisted his head, looked off into space for a moment then back to Mecana. "Met her a couple of months ago at Griffin's. Hit it off, and everything was cool until last week. Wanted me take her to a swingers party. You know, group sex, everybody fuckin' everybody. Not this dude. I do my fuckin' in private, so I split."

"I don't believe you," Mecana said.

"Why you think they call her Kinky, man? She's into that sort of thing."

"You're lying," Mecana shoved DeMax and he stumbled backwards and fell down.

DeMax rolled over and looked up at Mecana. "Check it out, man. I'm not the only one who knows."

"I will," Mecana said. "Get up." Mecana reached down, grabbed DeMax's arm and pulled him to his feet. The lady in the Ford shook her head and drove on down the street.

"Where were you last Monday night?" Rustin asked.

"My new girlfriend's place. There all night."

"What's her name and address?" Mecana asked.

"Judy Blackwell, 1342 East Cross Street. Got a roommate, too. Her name's Sara Moore. She was there from about midnight on that night. Don't know nothin' about what happened to Kinky, man, I swear."

"We'll see," Mecana said.

"You know a Julie Crawford, DeMax?"

"Not that I remember."

"You didn't know she was one of the victims?" Mecana said.

"Nope."

"We may need to talk to you again, DeMax," Rustin said. "We didn't see any open warrants on you but we could probably find one if we looked hard enough especially if you don't cooperate."

"You sure you're not dealing, DeMax?" Mecana said.

"Ain't goin' there, man."

"Let me rephrase that," Mecana said. "That Harley didn't come out of a Cracker Jack box. You've been picked up for drugs before. How you get your money?"

"I deliver pizzas for Big Top Pizza; pick up some money at Griffin's when they need an extra bartender. That how I met Kinky."

"You don't seem like the intellectual type, DeMax," Rustin said. "If you're not dealing, how come you're hanging out at a college bar?"

"Same reason any guy would - pussy. Lots of it and a lot of those rich white college chicks got money like Kinky. They like us brothers 'cause we got a little extra, if you know what I mean."

Mecana and Rustin looked at each other. There wasn't much they could say to that.

Mecana took the handcuffs off DeMax.

"Remember, DeMax, you be around if we need you. You got it?" Rustin said.

"Yeah. Got it. Think I broke some'n on my Harley. You goin' to pay for it? Your fault."

Rustin and Mecana grinned at each other. "I don't think so," Rustin said as they walked toward the Explorer.

"What you think, Mecana?" Rustin asked.

"If I was a betting man I would say no. This guy's mostly a street crook and cock hound. I don't think he's into that sort of thing. Of course, that's just what I think. I've been wrong before; we'll have more to go on when we get the lab results. We might pay them a visit and see where they are with it."

"Good, I'm anxious to know what killed them," Rustin said.

8

Mecana and Rustin drove over to have a look at the evidence. They got off the elevator on the sixth floor, walked through double doors with 'County Medical Examiner' printed on them. A tall, thin man wearing a white coat with 'David Seymour, MD' on it stepped out into the hall from his office in front of Mecana and Rustin.

"I was going to call you," the doctor said. "Your timing's perfect."

"Naturally, Doc," Mecana said and smiled. "This is Rustin Kemp, Doctor Seymour, he's from Houston. He's the one that found the Belmont girl."

"I hope what I've got helps," Doctor Seymour said, looking at Rustin.

Doctor David Seymour was in his fifties, gray hair, ramrod straight. He walked like he had a corn cob up his ass. The veterans called him Doctor Frankenstein. Today was business as usual.

He sat down with Rustin and Mecana at the conference table, laid a large folder on a table and opened it. He placed his pencil point on a picture. "You see the incision here," he said, "the vagina was removed by someone who knew precisely what he was doing. The cut runs from the urinary bladder to the rectum. Maybe he did it to collect a grotesque trophy. I don't know what other reason he could have for doing it."

"I've heard that terrible stuff before, Doc," Rustin said.

"It could be the same person," Seymour said.

"So, we may be looking for a doctor," Rustin said.

"Possible, or someone that knows a lot about female anatomy," Seymour replied. "I looked at the evidence of the murdered girl in Houston and the Crawford girl, also. It's not like a signature, but all three were done by skilled hands."

"That's a gruesome thought," Rustin said and cringed. "Did all of them die from the same thing?"

"They died from an overdose of tricyclic antidepressant. Better known as Ludimocson. The drug is out-dated, not prescribed anymore, but if someone had a supply. It would probably still be effective if it was sealed. I am convinced that whoever administered the drug knew its makeup. The effect is increased with the addition of alcohol. They were legally drunk when the drug was induced into their system. The Crawford girl had bicarbonate of soda in her blood. That increases the effect. She probably died quicker than the other two."

"How long did it take to kill them, Doc?" Mecana asked.

"Well, I can't say for sure, everyone's different, but they would have encountered blurred vision almost immediately. Gender has an effect. Estrogen in the female body speeds the effect. They would have had hallucinations and became disorientated shortly after the blurred vision, along with a number of other problems, before passing out. All of them probably died shortly after the drug was injected. If he wanted to keep any one of them alive longer," Seymour said, "he could have administered the drug in smaller quantities, and still have had a lethal dose if it was done in less than twenty-four hours. I think that may have been the case with the Belmont girl. They found several needle marks on her."

"Not only did this nut kill them," Mecana said, "but he knew it was the perfect drug to conceal his identity and render them helpless."

"Yes," Doctor Seymour said. "He knew what he was doing."

"I know this sounds ghoulish, Doc," Rustin said, "but do you think they could have been alive when they were mutilated?"

"No. The incision was too exact and smooth. Someone alive would have moved, the cut would have been jagged in some places. There's no sign of that here. There also wasn't any semen in any of them, and the vagina being removed left a lot of trauma to the abdominal cavities. Without semen and the other entire trauma to the body, I can't tell for sure if they were raped.

"The guy may have used a condom, or couldn't have sex. That may be part of his problem. One thing he did, though, was make sure he didn't leave any DNA."

"I know," Mecana said. "I checked out the cab driver, and the cab Kinky was in. The forensic boys also didn't find anything in the apartments of either girl. The bed was still made in both apartments; they never got home. I've talked to neighbors, friends and family. Nothing they didn't know each other, but they were beautiful, rich and liked to party. That has to tell us something, but so far I don't know what. You think the same person did all the killings, Doc?"

"I can't say with certainty; but from the evidence, I would say yes."

"This helps a lot, thanks," Mecana said.

"Where do you want me to send the lab bill, somebody has to pay for this, we can't."

"Send it to the Warfield Police Department, attention Chief David Orr," Mecana said.

"Okay. I'll let you know if I come up with anything else," Doctor Seymour said.

"Thanks, Doc, we'll see you later," Mecana said.

Doctor Seymour nodded, picked up the folder and left.

9

The sign on the door said 'Kevin E. Johnson - Hospital Administrator.' Diplomas from four different universities hung on the wall behind a large desk in a den-sized office with shiny hardwood floors. To the right of the desk - a big, closed, draped window hid a view of the hospital parking lot from the fourth floor. Seated at the desk was a neatly groomed six-foot forty-plus man with thinning blond hair. He was dressed in an expensive-looking brown suit tailored to fit his trim body. He glared intently at the two men seated on the other side of the desk for a couple of moments then spoke. "My secretary said you were policeman," he said. "What can I do for you gentleman?"

"Mr. Johnson, I'm Detective Thomas Mecana and this is my associate, Rustin Kemp. He's a former detective from Houston. We have been investigating the murders of three young women who-"

"Were they the ones they found in the river?" Johnson interrupted. "I read something about that."

"Two of them," Mecana said. "The first was in Houston. We believe they were all murdered by the same person. The evidence indicates that person could be a doctor, more specifically, a specialist like a gynecologist. We discovered a Doctor Dawson Durant took up residency here last October. He's the only GYN in the Dallas area that would have been in Houston at the time of the first murder. The murder victim in Houston was also a patient of his and was murdered on property owned by his father-in-law. We plan to spend some time checking out Doctor Durant and we wanted you to know."

"Are you saying you suspect Doctor Durant of theses crimes?"

"Let's just say he's a person of interest," Rustin said. "I am sure you have heard that before."

"Yes, I must say I am shocked. I don't know Doctor Durant well but his credentials are excellent. I know about the two frivolous lawsuits. We determined they were invalid before we let him come here. My nurses think he's extremely good-looking. I had one nurse say she would volunteer to be examined by him anytime he wanted." Johnson cut off a quick laugh and became serious again. "It seems unbelievable that he would be involved."

"He's probably not," Mecana said. "But life's full of surprises, so we have to cover all the bases. Whoever is murdering these young women does some hideous things to them. We have to stop him."

"Yes, I understand. Is there anything you would have me do?"

"No," Rustin said. "We wanted you to know when you saw us around why we were here. If it's alright with you we'll pretend to be maintenance employees. That gives us access to go anywhere."

Johnson nodded in agreement.

"Doctor Durant may not have had a thing to do with the murders, but he was in the right place at the right time. One of the murdered women was a patient of his. He was accused of sexual harassment by two of his former nurses and he is a GYN. All of that makes for an interesting combination. We'll need you to get his personal file for us."

Johnson leaned back in his chair and rubbed his chin. "The employee thing is okay but I'll need a court order to let you have his file."

"I'll get you one." Mecana said.

"Should I restrict his patient base?"

"No. We don't want to spook him," Mecana said. "Keep it business as usual. We'll have a tail on him for the next two weeks, at least. Don't do anything that might raise his suspicions."

"Is that it, Detective?" Johnson asked, and stood up from his desk. "I have a meeting I must attend."

Rustin and Mecana stood up. "That's it for now," Rustin said. "Thank you for your time. We will let you know what the outcome is."

"Good," he said and walked out from behind the desk.

"We can find our way out," Mecana said.

Johnson nodded and left the door open as he walked out of his office.

10

Chief Orr was going through speeding tickets from the night before when Mecana walked in. He stopped and gave Mecana a sour look. "What the hell are you doing having the examiner send me the lab invoice?" Orr asked. "Where do you think I am going to get the money? The budget they give me barely covers the salaries and the light bill."

"They're your murders, happened in your town. I couldn't very well send it to Dallas. There helping you out now by paying my salary. Which isn't enough, but that's another story. Write more tickets."

"I got two of the councilmen on my ass now because one of my dumbass patrolmen wrote their wives speeding tickets."

"You'll figure it out," Mecana said. "I need to set up a stakeout. Need two of your boys to help me."

"For how long?"

"Don't know."

"How am I going to write more tickets to pay for this bill if you take my guys away?"

"Write some yourself, instead of hanging out at the Beef Master."

"Who is this guy you want to watch?"

"His name's Doctor Dawson Durant."

Orr looked puzzled. "A doctor? You've got to be kidding."

"Nope. If he does anything suspicious, call me. Make sure he doesn't ID them or give them the slip. Here's a folder with his info and pictures. Be careful," Mecana dropped the folder on Orr's desk. "Me and Kemp will help you."

"I thought you didn't want Kemp on this?" Orr said.

"That was before I knew him. Brief your boys and be ready to go when I give you the word."

"I'll send Goodman home to get some sleep," Orr said. "Skinner can take first shift. He doesn't come in until 5 P.M. anyway."

"Whatever, just get it done," Mecana said.

"What makes you think it's a doctor, Mecana?"

"It's a long story. One I don't have time to tell you now."

"Alright, it's your call," Orr said.

"Good. Remember, don't try to arrest him without backup, no matter what he's done. You got me?"

"Yeah I got you," Orr said and reached for a Twinkie.

"Have you ever considered going to the gym and working a little of that fat off? You would feel better," Mecana said.

"What, and give up my standing in the Fat Man's Club?" Orr laughed and took a bite of Twinkie.

Mecana shook his head and left.

11

Mecana made contact with a real estate company to use an empty building not too far from the Durant Mansion as a lookout post. For the first three days, watching Durant was very routine. He got up, went to work and came home.

A stakeout could be one of the most boring things a cop could do. Sometime the boredom made you think too much. It was starting out that way for Rustin tonight. He couldn't get Debbie off his mind.

He parked behind Mecana's car, grabbed his flashlight and went in the 'For Lease' building to a big room with a clear view of the mansion several hundred yards away. "All quiet?"

"Not much to report," Mecana said. "He got home about six. His wife left soon after in the Lexus for somewhere. He's been in the house ever since. May have gotten lost in that place. It's as big as a hotel. Why would anyone want to live in something like that?"

"To impress. Show how rich they are," Rustin said.

Rustin bent down and took a look through the mounted binoculars on a tripod. "This guy has been a model citizen so far," he said. "We may be barking up the wrong tree."

"You never know."

Rustin's thoughts jumped back to his wife. "Mecana, you married?"

"Been divorced ten years. Spent too much time doing this sort of thing."

"I will be soon," Rustin said. "My wife left me. I think it was out of frustration more than anything. She didn't know how to deal with what happened to me. And I didn't have the patience to help her understand."

"Sometimes it's impossible to know why they do things," Mecana said. "In my case, it was easy to figure out. I took her for granted. Didn't spend enough time with my family or show them how much I loved them. The job came first. I was an asshole."

"I've been thinking about that," Rustin said. "After this is over, I think I'm going to get into another line of work. One that lets me come home at five and take the weekends off. Maybe she will take me back."

"This shit gets in your blood, buddy. You get hooked on the adrenaline rush when you take a bad guy down or save a potential victim. You'll just wind up making you both unhappy."

"Maybe, but maybe not," Rustin said. "Why don't you call it a night, Mecana, I'll watch our boy. If anything happens I'll let you know."

"Alright. Hey, I'm sorry about what I said. If you think that will save your marriage that's what you should do. Call me if you need me."

"Will do. See you in the morning," Rustin said.

"One of Orr's boys will relieve you. I got to go to the office in the morning to brief the Chief. Call if you need me."

12

About eight-thirty that evening, Durant came out of the house wearing jeans, a pull-over red sweater and a brown suede jacket. Not the attire he generally wore when he went to the hospital. He got in his BMW and headed toward town, Rustin following. Instead of making a right turn for the hospital, he drove on by and hit the freeway toward Dallas.

The traffic was light. Durant pushed the BMW up to speeds of ninety and hundred. It was all Rustin could do to keep him in sight.

He slowed down about five miles down the freeway turned off an exit over a railroad track, into an old neighborhood with small brick and frame houses. He pulled over and stopped in front of a small brick house with a chain link fence around it; no car in the drive. He cut the BMW off, walked up on the porch to the front door, took a key out of his pocket and went in. A light came on in the house.

Rustin drove on by, turned around, cut his lights and pulled up to the curb a block away. He took his .38 out of its holster and placed his hand on the door handle. Images of the Belmont girl popped up in front of him like a billboard and he froze, dropped the gun in the floorboard and began to shake. He fumbled for his pain killers in his pocket, grabbed some pills and poked them in his mouth, swallowed and looked at the house. There wasn't time to call for backup, just like before. He pushed on the door handle again and the door swung open. A chill ran through him. He felt the knife, the pain, the blood soaking his back again. It was so real he threw up and slammed the door. He couldn't do it. He punched the re-dial on his phone and Mecana answered.

"I can't do it. I can't. I tried, but I can't," Rustin said, his hands shaking.

"What the hell are you talking about, Rustin?"

"I'm in Dallas. I think I found his killing place, but I need help."

"What's the address? I'll send a SWAT team."

"1422 South Novel," Rustin said, looking at the street sign.

"I'm on my way. If he leaves, follow, and let me know where. It's alright, we'll get him. Stay in the car."

Rustin shook uncontrollably. All he could see was Linda Belmont's eyes pleading for help.

Durant was still in the house, and he couldn't do a thing.

Five minutes later, he heard approaching sirens. Four squad cars and an armored wagon came flying down the street. Rustin slid down in the seat. Officers surrounded the house. People were running out into the streets from nearby houses in panic. Some were jumping in their cars and hauling ass. A big black guy with a hooded jacket came charging out of the house across the street firing a pump shotgun at the police, they had to take him down.

Durant appeared at the door. A spotlight hit him and someone tossed a tear gas canister on the porch. Two SWAT team members, wearing gas masks, rushed in and knocked him to the floor. One put an assault rifle to his head. The other one handcuffed him. They jerked him to his feet and rushed him to a nearby cruiser and shoved him in the back seat.

Cops ran in the house from front and back. A couple minutes later, they came out with an old white-haired man wrapped in a blanket. His hands shaking, his eyes rolling around like marbles. An ambulance showed up shortly afterward. The dead black guy was put in the ambulance, the old white-haired man in a squad car, and they all left. It was all over in less than ten minutes. Several of the locals were still roaming around the street in a daze, wondering what the hell just happened.

13

Two men were standing inside a glass-paneled office, talking and gesturing at each other. One was Tom Mecana and the other one Assistant Police Chief for Homicide Robert Verves, a five-foot-six black man with a voice like the Jolly Green Giant.

From outside the office, the only thing you could tell for sure was they were mad. From the inside all hell was breaking loose.

"What were you thinking, Mecana, letting a civilian attempt to arrest a suspect that you didn't have any reason to be after in the first place?" Verves said, placing both hands on his desk, shaking his shaved black head like a bobblehead doll.

"He's not a civilian. He's a trained combat solider, a certified police officer for the State of Texas and a licensed private eye."

"All of which does not qualify him to be on this case," Verves said. "On top of that, you tell me he panicked and you had to rescue him!"

"It wasn't a rescue. It was providing backup like we're supposed to."

"To arrest a man that went to his grandfather's house to check on him? Come on, Mecana, let's get real."

"He was under surveillance. Rustin didn't know that. Why the hell is a doctor's grandpa living in a place like that anyway?"

"Because it's his home. He has lived there for forty years. That's why the good doctor transferred his practice to Dallas to take care of the old man until he died. Did it ever occur to you to check that out?"

"No, not really," Mecana ran his hand through his hair.

"Well I did. There was no way he could have committed the Houston murder. He was in Los Angeles for a seminar. And it looks like he was with his brother when the Crawford girl was killed. Not sure about the Sadler murder yet, but it looks like you're way off track."

"I wouldn't be too sure of that. I've seen a lot of arranged alibis."

"We could be in deep shit over this, Mecana."

"For doing our job?"

"You didn't do it right."

"You want this damn badge?" Mecana took his badge off and slammed it on the desk, then turned to walk out.

"No, hard head, I don't want your badge. I think we dodged a bullet. I told the doctor we were there to arrest the shooter from across the street and mistakenly went to the wrong house. I think he bought it. We may have got lucky and avoided a lawsuit as big as Mount Rushmore. The guy we took down was wanted for murder. He thought we were there for him. We sure as hell can't afford to have Kemp on this anymore. You understand, Mecana?"

"Rustin Kemp has been though hell," Mecana said. "I don't know if I could have handled it any better if I had been through the same."

"Mecana, I can sympathize with the boy. I want the murderer caught just as bad as he does. But we can't let Kemp continue on the case. You can let him be an advisor. Talk to him about the case, but he can't be out in the field with us. He will get us both fired, and maybe even get himself killed."

Mecana let out a big sigh and shook his head. "As much as I hate to admit it, I know you're right, Chief."

"Alright then, lets move on, enough about that," Verves said. "Do you know Darcie Connors?"

"No, should I?" Mecana asked.

"She's been working on the abused wife case we just wrapped up. Good cop."

"What are you telling me, Chief?"

"She's your new partner, like it or not."

"Well, it's not, but I know when to eat crow. Could use some help keeping an eye on Griffin's."

"What I thought. I have already talked to the owner. He knows to keep it quiet. We'll have her go to work there as a waitress. Here's her number, call her so you two can get acquainted."

"Okay, in the meantime I'll keep an eye on the doctor. There's something about that dude that's not right."

"What did I tell you, Mecana? Leave the guy alone. It's not him."

"I'll make it very indiscreet."

"You're going to give me an ulcer, Mecana. I should fire you now."

"Your call, Chief."

"Go away, let me die in peace," Verves sat down in his chair and put his head in his hands.

Mecana grinned, blew Verves a kiss, and walked out of the office.

14

Mecana had on his US Marines sweatshirt, gym shorts and running shoes, going nowhere on a treadmill. There was something calming to Mecana about working up a sweat in the gym. It energized him and cleared his head. He needed a clear head right now. He had asked Rustin Kemp to meet him at the gym. He got there early to work off his frustrations and think about what he was going to say to Rustin.

Rustin had put him back on the right path when he wanted to quit, now he was going to have to tell him to quit. Maybe he should hang it up, too, and let someone else give Verves an ulcer. The difference was Rustin may still have a shot at saving his marriage and a future if he quit. He didn't have anything but unemployment. He was nothing without his badge.

He elevated the treadmill and increased his speed. An overweight guy next to him looked at Mecana's muscular body, smiled and cranked his treadmill up.

Rustin came in and saw Mecana on the treadmill. He shuffled over to him, looked at Mecana and grinned.

Mecana cut the treadmill, got off, picked up a towel and wiped his sweaty face.

The fat guy cut his treadmill, staggered over to a chair and sat down, huffing and puffing.

"There was a time I would have kicked your butt good in a gym," Rustin said. "Was a quarterback - a damn good one. Then I quit college and got married. My old man wanted me to be a pro. But you know how it is, love conquers all, or some garbage like that. Next thing I know I'm chasing a crackhead down an alley and discover Linda Belmont about to die, and I almost did. How do you explain something like that?"

"You don't," Mecana said. "It's like when you're driving down a county road and a squirrel runs out in front of you. One second sooner, or one second later, and he lives to be an old nut-gathering squirrel. But that's not what happened. Why was it you? Why at that precise moment? Why that squirrel? There's not a reason for it, it's a thing called fate. That's what life is. We're all victims of fate, good and bad."

"Well, it sure has some lingering effects."

"That's why I asked you to come by. I have something to tell you. You deserve to hear it without the candy-coating I had planed on. The other night's events had some lingering effects. The doctor may try to sue the city. My boss is pretty upset. I'm going to have to ask you to go home and let me take care of this. We fucked up and they're making you the scapegoat. It's just as much my fault as yours, but they want you to take the fall. I offered my badge but it didn't make any difference. It's probably for the best. You said you were going get into something else. Go home, and start over with your wife."

"I can't go home. I will have to do it by myself," Rustin said. "I wasn't prepared for the emotional consequences of the other night. I am now. It won't happen again. I don't have a life until I can put this thing behind me. I have to find the killer of that young lady. It's my fault she's dead."

"I don't think you were listening, Rustin. You have no authority here. They will put your ass in jail. Then what will you do? You can stick around if you want, I'll keep you informed. But you can't get in the way of this case."

"Mecana, I know you went to bat for me. I appreciate that. But I have to do this. I know that may be hard for you to understand but I don't have a choice. I have nothing else."

"I know what you're saying, but there's nothing I can do. My hands are tied," Mecana wiped his face again; Houston tossed the towel over his shoulder. "Sorry, headed for the shower."

15

Mecana was walking toward his truck in the parking lot when his phone rang. It was Rustin.

"Mecana, I want you to find that bastard for me. You're right, I can't do it alone. I'm not able. The best thing for me to do is check out."

"Where you going?"

"To hell, probably," he said and was gone.

Mecana stared at his phone in thought. "What the hell did he mean by that?" Mecana thought. "Damn, he's going to kill himself."

He attempted to call Rustin three times, but no answer. He fired up the Silverado and took off like Silver for the Sunset Motel.

Mecana saw Rustin's Explorer parked in front of Room 38. The room was dark. He cut the Silverado off, got out and rushed to the door, knocked; no answer.

Then he yelled, "Rustin, you in there?" Still no answer. He raised his leg and kicked the door as hard as he could and it flew open. Rustin was lying on the floor beside the bed, fully clothed but unconscious. Mecana flipped the lights on and bent down and checked Rustin's pulse. He was breathing. He looked for wounds and saw none; he dialed 911. A few minutes later, an ambulance arrived, put Rustin on a ventilator, and he rode to the hospital with him.

After two hours, a tired-looking young black doctor came out and asked if anyone was with Rustin Kemp.

"I am," Mecana said.

"I'm Doctor Kelly. Mr. Kemp took an overdose of pain killers. He had an empty prescription bottle in his pocket. We pumped his stomach and put him on an IV. He had three times the amount of the drug in his system that he should have. If you had not found him when you did he would have died. We will keep him for a couple of days, make sure there's no further complications before we release him. He may need treatment if it was intentional. You can talk to him about that."

Mecana camped in Rustin's hospital room until he woke up. When he did he was drowsy and confused. "Where the hell am I?" Rustin asked, wide-eyed.

"You're in a hospital. You did a foolish thing. Let's don't do that again. It takes too much out of me."

"Oh yeah, I remember. Figured the world was better off without me."

"Hey, no skin off my ass, but you're the one that told me not to give up. You disappointed me."

"Don't have much to live for," Rustin said.

"That's a shitty answer. What about your family, your wife?"

"My wife could care less."

"I don't think so. I found her number in your wallet and called her. She should be here any time. You need to get your damn act together, buddy boy, and quit feeling sorry for yourself. There's a lot of people worse off than you are. Besides, we got a killer to catch."

"You had no right to call my wife."

"Then who does? You do this 'poor pitiful me' bit and everyone is supposed to ignore it? I don't think so. You want me to butt out, fine, but have the guts to face your problems. Let me know when you grow a backbone." Mecana got up, pushed the chair back angrily and left.

A nurse walked in and stuck a thermometer in Rustin's mouth and wrapped a blood pressure strap around his arm.

"I wish to hell everybody would leave me alone. They don't have to live in my skin,

I don't want to live any more."

"Mr. Kemp, everything is going to be alright," the nurse said.

"No, it's not. Go away," he said.

"Your blood pressure is going sky high; you're going to have to calm down," the nurse said.

"Get the hell out!"

The nurse backed off with a frightened look. "I'll go get the doctor," she said and left.

16

Debbie walked in the room, dressed in a blue sweater and jeans. Her long blonde hair resting on her shoulders, she looked like she could still be a cheerleader if she wanted to.

She looked at Rustin, then took a depth breath "Mr. Mecana said you needed me."

Rustin nervously looked at Debbie. He wanted to jump out of the bed and take her in his arms and kiss her passionately, but he wasn't sure she would want him to. "Mr. Mecana should mind his own business," he said.

"You want me here or not?"

"Only if you want to be."

"I tried to help before but you shut me out. I felt like I didn't matter, our love didn't matter. You were only interested in what was happening to you. I couldn't take it any more."

"I thought you resented me for being a cripple; didn't love me."

"Rustin, I have loved you since I was six years old. You think I could just turn that off?"

"You think I'm nuts," he said.

"I think your feelings of guilt have got the best of you. But you're just as much a victim as she was, it's not your fault she's dead."

"If I had been the cop I should have been it would have never happened. I failed her. I'll never get over that."

"No one expects you to, but you can't destroy your life and mine because of it. We all make mistakes. Sometimes the consequences are horrible, but that's life. We don't know what our fate is," Debbie said.

"That's what Mecana said. Gave me some corny analogy about a squirrel."

"He's right. It's not the end of the world. I'm sorry for the lady and her family, but I'm sorry for us too. Life goes on, if you let it."

"I don't know what to say. I'm sorry for what I put you through," Rustin said.

The door opened and Doctor Kelly walked in. "Mr. Kemp, I'll take your vitals and if everything is okay, I'll remove your IV and you can go home. We're not going to keep you against your will. I don't have the authority to do that. But I can tell you, you need treatment," he said. "I can call the rehabilitation center for you if you want an appointment to have a psychiatrist get you into rehab. It's up to you."

Rustin looked at Debbie. Debbie smiled and nodded her head yes.

"Thank you," he said. "Please do that. The sooner the better."

"Very well. I'll remove the IV. Get dressed and I'll make the call."

PART TWO

17

Mecana stuck his Glock in the nightstand, went to bed and tossed and turned all night, thinking about Rustin, and his new partner. He was going to have to call her before Verves gave him another ass chewing.

He got up early, picked up a cup of coffee at Seven Eleven and stopped off at the hospital to check on Rustin. Before going to Psychiatrist Rupert P. Wyler's office, he went barreling into the room to discover a fat lady uncovered on the bed in a short nightgown.

The view was not a pretty sight.

He apologized as he backed out of the room then stopped at a nurse's station. They told him Rustin left with his wife and checked into the Fort Worth Addiction Clinic. Maybe the boy was going to be alright after all, he thought. A pudgy Hispanic receptionist was answering phone calls in English and Spanish in the outer office at Doctor Wyler's, as Mecana sat waiting his turn.

A reproduction of Norman Rockwell's 'Doctor/Little Boy' painting hung on one wall, a TV mounted on another had Wild Kingdom on. A lion chasing an antelope that was running for his life.

A middle-aged man in a business suit walked out of the doctor's office with a wild-eyed expression and disappeared out the front door.

The receptionist rose up from her desk and motioned for Mecana to go in.

A little man wearing a white shirt, red bowtie, blue suspenders and Einstein-looking bushy white hair with a matching mustache was engrossed in a paper he was reading. He pointed to a chair for Mecana to sit down without looking up, and kept reading. Mecana sat down and waited to be recognized like a schoolboy.

Doctor Wyler coughed and dropped the paper on his cluttered desk and looked at Mecana.

"I've been expecting you, Mecana. I was reading the examiner's report on the victims again. You've got a real dingbat this time," he made circler motions with his index finger.

"Looks like it, Doc. I-"

"Don't call me Doc. I hate that," he interrupted and shivered. "Rupert will be fine."

"Sorry, Rupert, didn't mean any disrespect."

"I just have a thing about it, gives me the willies. Now, what were you saying?" he asked, adjusting his bright blue suspenders.

"I was saying I hope you can give me some insight into what this nut's about."

Doctor Wyler leaned back in his chair and ran his hand through his bushy hair. "This one is something special. Schizophrenic most likely, and a chronic insomniac. I would suspect some kind of trauma at an early age. Perhaps a parent was murdered and mutilated, or he was the murderer.

Something that blew his mind into another orbit, where the monster now lives.

"He's probably perfectly normal most of the time. Then something triggers it, and he becomes this 'Jekyll and Hyde'-type person. People like him appear to be in control but, there's a storm brewing inside of them all the time, waiting to explode. I would think he would be an average size male in his late-thirties or early-forties. The drugs and knife indicate a need for added confidence. You might look at the drug. It's outdated. Where would he get it, or did he already have a supply? I understand why he's using it, fits his crime perfectly. The potency of a drug that old, I would question, but that's not my area of expertise."

"The Medical Examiner said he thought the drug would be effective if it was sealed," Mecana said.

"He should know," Wyler said.

"Anything else, Doc? Oh, sorry, Rupert."

"He'll continue to kill. Most likely using the same MO. The time between his first and second victim is a bit confusing. He may be trying to stop killing but can't. The bottom line is I would look for a highly educated person, not necessarily a doctor, but someone who has enough knowledge of female anatomy to perform surgery. That's part of the reason for the mutilations. He's proud of his skill, maybe more than a doctor would be. That's why he does it, and the possibility, of course, that it has something to do with a warped sexual fantasy. He may not be able to have sexual intercourse, and instead gets his 'jollies' from the murder and mutilation."

Doctor Wyler dug a folder off of his cluttered desk and handed it to Mecana. "This is my official report. It has some technical jargon in it, in case we have to go to court, but basically it's what I told you. It's only a question of time before he does it again, if you don't catch him."

"You confirmed what I already knew, Rupert. The trick is catching him."

"Alright, but I am still sending my bill to the city."

Mecana grinned, stood up with the folder, shook hands with Wyler and left.

He tossed the report on the truck seat and took a few minutes to work up the courage to call his new partner.

"Hi," he said. "This Darcie Connors?"

"Your ID say's Tom Mecana. I've been waiting for your call," she said.

"Thought we better meet, get started," Mecana said. "How about the Warfield Police Station around one-thirty this afternoon?"

"Good," she said. "See you there."

18

Mecana pulled up to the Warfield Police Station at one-twenty-five in the afternoon. A new black unmarked Charger was parked next to Orr's car. It had that Government Issue look. He assumed it belonged to Darcie Connors. When he walked in he wasn't prepared for what he saw. She was thirty-something, wearing a chic black dress with short, shiny black hair. Big, soft, brown eyes, delicious-looking red lips and a body designed for a man's temptation.

She must not have been there long because David Orr was still trying to get the smile off his face.

She spotted Mecana, glided toward him with hips swaying and high heels tapping out a three-quarter-time sonata on the hardwood floor.

Not what he expected at all. He waited for the lady to extend her hand. It was soft and smooth with long red nails.

He shook hands with her. "Tom Mecana," he said, holding on to her hand. "Been hearing good things about your work."

"I hear you're one of the best," she said, retrieving her hand. "It's a privilege to meet you."

Mecana gave her that 'aw shucks' look, gestured toward a chair for her to sit down and laid the profile on the table.

After Darcie was seated, he sat down and pointed to the folder. "Why don't you take that home and read it. Have you ever worked on a case like this?"

"No, mostly domestic cases. Still fighting the stigma of being a woman. That's why I wanted this case, gives me a chance to break the mold."

"We got a real sicko here," he said.

"You're the expert. I'll follow your lead. Tell me what you want me to do."

"Our best bet is to have you go undercover at Griffin's Bar and Grill. Do you have any family here?"

"No. Divorced, no kids. My family lives in Waco. I come from a long line of educators. Mom and Dad are retired school teachers A sister and a brother, both teachers."

"I'm divorced too," Mecana said. "Have two daughters in Austin, no family here. My old man's a retired Marine

Colonel. My mother's deceased. Have a brother that's a Marine Major. Not having family here takes some pressure off. Makes it less complicated. We only have to worry about each other."

"I'm ready to go," Darcie said and tapped the folder.

"Chief Verves set up a job for you at Griffin's. I'll follow you to work, and home after every shift, to make sure this nut hasn't figured out what we're doing. Keep a gun and phone handy at all times. If anything suspicious happens, let me know. Do not try to apprehend a suspect by yourself."

"When do we start?" she asked.

"How about tomorrow to give you time to read the profile and ask any questions you might have."

"Sounds good. I'm looking forward to working with you, Tom."

"Thanks. Call me Mecana, everyone does."

"Alright, Mecana," she said.

"How long you been a cop?" Mecana asked.

"A little over six years. Thought I wanted to be a lawyer. I didn't. After a couple years of practice and a divorce, I got bored, wound up being a cop."

"Okay, tomorrow. Let's meet at the McDonalds down the street, say eight-thirty. Being the big spender I am, I'll buy breakfast."

"My, you are gracious," Darcie smiled, got up and extended her soft hand again. They shook hands. She picked up the folder, waved at Chief Orr and was gone.

"Damn," Orr said. "If there had been lookers like that on the force when I was there I never would have left."

"She is pretty, isn't she," Mecana said.

"Pretty is not a strong enough word." Orr said.

Mecana had mixed emotions about his new partner, especially a woman. The last time he had a female partner she decided to break down crying right in the middle of a gun battle. This one sounded more confident. It wouldn't take long to find out.

"Orr, I want you and your men to be ready to assist us in case the killer shows up at Griffin's, and I don't want any excuses. You don't answer our call and I'll have you before the boys across the street to fire your ass," Mecana warned.

"Don't worry about us. We'll be there," Orr said.

"You damn well better be."

"Quit worrying, Mecana. I may not look the part but I know how to be a cop."

Mecana nodded and walked out the door.

19

Mecana made several suggestions on what aliases Darcie should use at Griffin's, none of which she liked. She applied some kind of female logic that Mecana didn't understand and said, "A woman has to like who she is even if that's not who she is."

"Yogi Berra would have been proud," Mecana mumbled to himself.

She finally decided on Linda Longstreet because she thought it sounded poetic.

She went to work the late shift, when the young ladies would be the most vulnerable. Mecana hung out at a nearby pool hall. He instructed Darcie to call immediately if anything suspicious happened. Nothing did for over a week. Both got red-eyed from loss of sleep.

On a Friday night the following week, at half past eleven, Mecana was about to take a shot at the eight ball, when Darcie called. She said she was watching the parking lot camera and a young woman left the bar alone and was being approached in the parking lot by a man with a knife.

"Call for back up, Darcie," Mecana said. "I'm on the way."

In less than three minutes, Mecana came speeding up in the Silverado and got out with his Glock in hand.

A big man wearing a hooded coat and jeans was trying to force a woman into an old blue Ford van at knifepoint. The man saw Mecana coming at him. The woman screamed and the man broke into a run across the parking lot, knocking a couple down as he ran by. He ran across another parking lot, into a clump of trees, and flung the knife and something else away. He tried to jump a four-foot-tall chain link fence, caught his heel and fell over to the other side. By the time he got to his knees, Mecana jumped the fence and had a gun pointed at his head.

"Police! Get on the ground, hands on your head!" Mecana jerked his coat back and showed the badge on his belt. The man hesitated. "Get down, asshole, last time before I blow your shit away!" The man looked at Mecana's cold gray eyes, got the message and lay down on the ground. Mecana squatted down, put his knee in the man's back, clamped handcuffs on him and searched him. He had an expired Nevada driver's license and some change in his pockets. His name was Luther Leroy Davidson, age thirty-four.

Two Warfield units came flying up beside him. Two officers got out, guns drawn.

Darcie came running up with her Beretta in one hand and her badge in the other. "We got him, Mecana," she said.

Mecana nodded, holstered the Glock, and worked on getting a deep breath.

The officers got Davidson to his feet and sat him down in the back of a squad car.

"He threw away the knife and something else back there," Mecana said. "Why don't you read him his rights, Darcie, I'll go look for it," Mecana said.

One of the officers overheard Mecana and pulled a Miranda Rights card out of his shirt pocket and handed it to Darcie. She walked over to the car and opened the door and looked in at Davidson.

"I'm going to read you your rights," she said.

"Fuck you, bitch!" he said, and scooted over in the seat away from her.

20

Darcie and Mecana were waiting in the conference room when Verves walked in. "Well, we got a bad guy, but not the one we were looking for. Luther Davidson served five years for attempted sexual assault. He was released from a Nevada prison last week. Didn't take him long to try it again. I turned the knife and crack over to property."

"I figured that out by the time I took him down," Mecana said. "Won't do any good to work Griffin's anymore. He will damn sure know what we're doing now."

"I agree," Verves said. "We have to widen our search. I'll try to hold off the press. The public is getting impatient. I can understand why. Go through the wrap sheets again, expand the search. There may be someone we overlooked before. Let me know if there's anything you need."

"We haven't run a check on the drug yet," Mecana said. "We need to do that. Find out if any doctors or medical personnel were being treated in Houston during the time the drug was being prescribed."

"I'll have the computer boys do that, let you know," Verves said. "Got to run. We can't leave a stone unturned. Find him."

"We'll do our best, Chief," Mecana said.

"That's all I can ask." He padded Mecana on the shoulder and left the room.

"I was reading about serial killers," Darcie said. "Most were flying under the radar before they were caught. People that appeared to be normal family men. They had their hobbies and extracurricular activities. Maybe this guy has a similar hobby to one of the known killers, that would give us a clue."

"Come on," Mecana said, mocking Darcie's comments. "Like I enjoy cutting up live chickens on the weekend to see them bleed, or roasting dogs over a camp fire, or being a clown like Gacy."

Darcie stared at Mecana, her dark brown eyes flashing. "What have you come up with besides checking drugs and a prominent doctor, Sherlock? We're no closer than when I joined this merry band."

Mecana shook his head, looked at the ceiling, then Darcie. "Sorry, Darcie. The guy is outsmarting us at every turn. I don't like that. It frustrates the living hell out of me."

"And you think it's Durant, in spite of his alibis?"

"Yep. Something about that guy's not right."

"Maybe so, but the chief said to expand our search with known sex offenders. Are you ready to do that?"

"Sure, I'm open to checking everything and everybody. Tell you what, let's start after lunch. I'll take you to someplace other than McDonalds. My treat."

Darcie smiled and shook her head at Mecana. "You are losing it."

"Not really. I thought I would take you to Brogans. They have a discount lunch special every Thursday." They both laughed.

21

After lunch, Mecana and Darcie checked files of known sex offenders, especially the ones with a history of violence.

Darcie ran the mouse on her computer down the page and something caught her eye. "I think I got something, Mecana," she said. "This guy's crime was fifteen years ago for rape and attempted murder. His name is Simon Carter. He's Caucasian, a former hospital orderly, forty-two-years-old. He was paroled a little over a year ago after serving seventeen years; that means he was on the street when the murders were committed."

"Yeah, let me see that." Mecana moved closer to Darcie and looked at the screen. "A parole board let him out for good behavior," he said. "That's like letting a rattlesnake back in the bushes. He left his victim for dead in a field after he stabbed and raped her." Mecana paused and grimaced. "My god, he stabbed her twenty times. Somehow she managed to crawl to the edge of the highway and a passing motorist saw her and called 911. She survived. Damn, that lady has guts. She even testified against him. He was given fifteen-to-life. The victim moved out of state after her testimony. His last known address was in the Dallas area. He's working at the Green Way Landscape Company as a laborer."

"How can supposedly-smart men and women let someone like that out on the street again?" Darcie asked. "It boggles my mind. Common sense would tell you no."

"You are naïve, partner, it's all about money - getting it and not getting it, depending on your agenda. Let's go have a talk with this rehabilitated citizen."

Mecana parked the Silverado in the space marked 'Visitor' and he and Darcie got out and went in a small portable building with an office sign.

A large lady with short brown hair was sitting in an oversized chair holding a phone to her ear; with a computer monitor on her desk, flashing a solitaire card game. A sign on her desk said 'SHIRLEY NEWMAN - MANGER.'

"I know the tree is blocking your driveway, Mr. Owens," she said, "but I can't get anyone out there until tomorrow." She jerked the phone away and rubbed her ear. "Jerk." She put the phone down. "I hope you don't have an emergency," she said, looking up at Mecana and Darcie. "The thunderstorm yesterday has got us running our tail off."

"No, nothing like that. We're from the police. We called you earlier to verify you have an employee by the name of Simon Carter. We need to have a talk with him."

She tried to cross her legs, couldn't and dropped her leg back down. "What now? One of you guys shows up every time there's a sex crime?"

"Yes we do. Where is he?" Mecana asked.

"He's with a crew on Early Street, off LBJ Freeway. Bunch of trees down, we're trying to clean it up."

"Thanks, we'll find it," Darcie said, and they turned to leave.

"Wait, I'll call him to come in, don't want the police going to my work site."

"Okay, but don't tell him we're here," Mecana said.

The fat lady nodded, picked up her phone and dialed. "Stormy, I need Carter in here now, I'll explain later," she said. "Have him take your truck and you come in with the crew." She punched the phone off and set it back on her desk. "Okay he's on his way."

An hour-and-a-half later, Carter still hadn't arrived.

"How long should it take for Carter to get here?" Darcie asked.

"Should have been here half hour ago," Shirley said.

"Has he got a phone, or one in the truck?" Darcie said.

"No, we use cell phones. Don't think he has one."

"He must have figured out what was going on," Mecana said. "You got the number of your truck?"

"Yeah, sure." She reached in a drawer and took out a copy of the registration and handed it to Mecana.

"Thanks, we'll let you know where your truck is when we find it. If he shows up, or you hear from him, let us know." Mecana handed her a card. "To be on the safe side, don't let him see that card or hear you call. If he wants to know why you had him come in, send him over to Mr. Owens' house," Mecana smiled.

Shirley smiled back. "I'll do that."

"You may need a new employee," Mecana said.

"Hope I don't need a new truck," she replied.

"Me too," Mecana said.

22

Mecana got on the radio and gave the dispatcher the license number of the Green Way truck, with a warning it may be stolen and that the man driving is a parolee by the name of Simon Carter. "He could be armed and dangerous." Mecana requested back up to 1457 North Maple as soon as possible. He would be waiting. "No sirens. I repeat, no sirens."

"Why would he run before we talk to him?" Darcie asked.

"Fear, for whatever reason. The crimes we're investigating, another one, or going back to prison; I would think any one of the three would do it. We'll go to his house. If he's running, he may go there to get whatever he considers important before he bugs out."

The white and green Green Way pickup was sitting in the driveway. No one was in it.

Mecana parked on the street a block away. "Well, we know we got the right address," he said.

"Should we wait for back up?" Darcie asked.

"Yes, but let's get in position before he knows anyone is here. When the back up arrives, we'll go in after him."

Mecana motioned for Darcie to go around to the back. She nodded and drew her Beretta. Mecana took a position beside the door, drew his Glock and waited for Darcie to get in place.

Two cruisers came roaring up, making all kinds of noise. The cops jumped out, drew their revolvers and leaned over the hood, pointing them at the door.

Mecana held his badge up. "Must be rookies," he said to himself. He made a downward motion with his arm for the uniforms to lower their weapons and they did.

"Carter, it's the police," Mecana spoke into the speaker. "Come out with your hands in the air."

No answer.

"Come out of there, Carter. Now. We need to talk, you're not under arrest."

Still no answer.

Mecana motioned for a cop to move to the back of the house to join Darcie; the other one to stay put. He holstered his Glock, stepped back and kicked the lock off, and the door opened and swung inside the house. Mecana drew his gun again and ran in the house, the cop right behind him. Darcie and the other cop busted in the backdoor. They moved through the house room by room, still no one. Darcie saw a light under a basement door and pointed it out. Mecana tried to turn the doorknob, but it was locked. Again, he stepped back, only this time he kept the Glock in his hand and gave a big kick to the door. The wood splintered. The door came open, bullets whizzed by his head and he dropped down on the floor.

"Get back!" he yelled to Darcie and the young cops.

The windows of the room were covered with black paint. There was a single overhead light. A rugged-looking man with a shaved head had a rifle pointed at Mecana and a knife stuck in his belt. He was standing in front of a naked girl with a chain around her ankle tied to the wall. Her hands cuffed behind her back, a ball gag in her mouth tied around her head.

"Drop the gun Carter, now!" Mecana said. Darcie and the cops were crouched beside the door.

Carter raised the rifle to fire again. Mecana put three quick rounds in his left shirt pocket. He dropped the rifle and fell to all fours, blood spilling out across the floor. He looked at Mecana, reached for the rifle with a blood covered trembling hand, made a painful moan and fell to the floor with a thud.

The girl was screaming hysterically, but the sound was muffled by the gag, saliva trickling out the sides of her mouth. Her big blue eyes rolling around like a pinball machine. She looked like an attractive blonde teenager, maybe fourteen or fifteen, small cuts and bruises all over her body.

Darcie came rushing in and wrapped her coat around the girl, holding her. She stared at Darcie, her blue eyes wide with fear. Darcie started talking to her. "You're alright. You're safe, were cops."

The hysterical girl collapsed to the floor, Darcie sliding down with her, holding the coat around her. She rolled her eyes back in her head and passed out.

"Call an ambulance," Darcie said to the young cop.

Mecana checked Carter. He was dead. He holstered his Glock and moved over to Darcie and the girl. "How's she doing?"

"She needs a doctor."

"The ambulance is on the way," Mecana said.

"How did he know?" Darcie asked, her arms around the unconscious girl.

"Don't know. Being called in may have never happened before, and having the girl here made him suspicious," Mecana said.

"I think we got our killer, Mecana," Darcie said.

"Don't know. One thing's for sure, he won't do it again."

Darcie looked down at the unconscious girl. "Poor thing. Hope she's okay."

"Yeah, looks like she's been through a hell of an ordeal. Go get some cutters out of your car, officer," Mecana said to the young cop. "Let's get this damn stuff off her."

The cop nodded and left the room.

Mecana looked around the room at the mattress on the floor, two sets of shackles, and various sex toys on a table with a stack of porno magazines. An assortment of food trash was piled in the corner. The strong smell of urine filled the room.

"You know, Darcie, she's not the only one that's been in this room. No telling what he's done here. I don't know how they do it, but people like him seem to have some kind of radar for spotting troubled kids."

"Unfortunately, it's a sick world," Darcie said. "I wish that damn ambulance would get here. This kid's shaking like a leaf."

"They will be here in a minute. From the way you're mothering that kid you might reconsider having some," Mecana said.

"I don't think so. I'm doing what has to be done," she said.

23

Mecana and Darcie arrived at headquarters a little after nine. Verves was writing something on a notepad when they walked in.

"Morning. You two okay?" he asked.

"I think so," Mecana said. "What did you find out about the girl?"

"A fifteen-year-old runaway from Florida. Her name's Suzann Micelles. She's going to be okay, or at least okay physically. She said she met Carter at a hamburger joint, where she went to spend her last dollar for something to eat about two months ago. He played the fatherly bit and told her he had a room she could stay in. He's had her tied up at his house ever sense, raping her at his leisure. You found her just in time. He told her he was tired of her and would have to get rid of her; that was two days ago. She was overdue.

We searched his house from top to bottom. Unfortunately, nothing in his house or any personal effects ties him to any of the mutilator murders. According to Greenway, he was two hundred miles away on a job when the Freeman girl was killed. The only drugs were a small amount of crack. These nuts keep showing up, but it's like winning the lottery, and being disappointed at the amount. We're taking some bad guys off the street, but we haven't found the worst of all."

"Damn," Darcie said. "I was hoping there would be a connection and we had him."

"Yeah, me too," Mecana said, "but I realized his MO didn't fit."

"As they say, back to the drawing board," Verves said.

"Chief, you think we should continue to look at the wrap sheets?" Darcie asked.

"Wouldn't hurt, but I don't have too much faith in you finding anything else."

"Me neither," Mecana said. "From the way this whole thing is going down I think we're dealing with a first time criminal, a very sick one, but someone that doesn't have a criminal record."

"Like a doctor," Darcie said and looked at Mecana.

"Yes, a doctor. Like Dawson Durant. He would be smart enough to not leave any DNA because he knows how it works, and the drug is his kind of thing."

"We've been down this road before, Mecana," Verves said. "The doctor has alibis that have been checked and re-checked. It's time you moved away from that and approached this with an open mind."

"I can do that, but I want to be certain first."

Verves looked at Darcie. "Maybe you can talk some sense into him. I don't seem to be getting anywhere. Instead of an open mind, he's got a one track mind."

"I'm the junior partner here. I'm following his lead. I just hope whoever it is makes a mistake and we catch him before it happens again."

"There's some kind of plan to the murders," Mecana said. "That's why I keep coming back to Durant. Somewhere in this puzzle is the answer to who, and why, they all have a connection to Durant. I think he's the one to answer it."

"I don't think so," Verves said. "But you seem to have a sixth sense for these sorts of things, so I won't rule it out completely. Get back to work and keep me posted."

24

Shortly after Mecana and Darcie left, Lineal Crawford showed up at Verve's office unannounced. He was tall and slim, had salt and pepper hair with a salon cut, a tailored gray suit that fit his slim body perfectly, a hand painted tie and custom made shoes.

"Chief Verves, my name's Lineal Crawford. I'm an attorney. I represent the Lamonts and the Durants. I'm also the father of Julie."

"I know who you are, counselor," Verves said.

"I'm here to have you remove Thomas Mecana from the mutilator case. He's constantly harassing my clients, and there's no proof they were involved in any way."

"Mr. Crawford, are you serious? I've been on this job for almost twenty years and I have never seen anyone as cold. Your daughter was brutally murdered and you're here because of some rich folks? Let me ask you one question: What if Mecana is right? How are you going to live with that?"

"He's not. I have known the Lamonts for twenty years, they're good people."

"I don't condone everything Mecana does, Crawford, but he is one of the best homicide detectives I have ever seen. Until I am told by my boss, or a court order, he stays on the case."

"Very well, if that's what it takes. I'll see if I can accommodate you, and include you in the process," Crawford said.

"Whatever, Mr. Crawford," Verves said.

"Mr. Verves, Mecana has been abusing his authority for years; it's about time someone did something about it. He killed that kid two years ago and nobody did anything."

"The internal affairs board cleared him. It was self defense," Verves said.

"So you say," Crawford added.

"That kid, as you call him, Mr. Crawford, was twenty-three-years-old and wanted for murder. He was pointing a gun at Mecana. If Mecana had hesitated one more second he would have been dead. He was defending himself against a cold-blooded killer. People like you make me sick to my stomach. You don't even care what happened to your own flesh and blood. It's all about money. Get out of my office!"

"You'll be hearing from me, Verves," Crawford said and walked out.

Verves stood there like a statue, looking at the door Crawford went out, then mumbled, "I told you you were going to give me an ulcer, Mecana."

25

Cindy Freeman was an attractive, petite twenty-five-year-old flight attendant who shared a condo with her boyfriend ten miles from the DFW Airport. He was on a two-day flight to California and Washington.

She had just returned from a turnaround to Chicago, arriving back in Dallas at one in the morning. She drove home, punched the garage door remote, pulled into the garage, pressed the button again and watched as the door dropped down and settled on the garage floor. Her boyfriend had cautioned her about being secure. She cut the engine on her black five-year-old Corvette, got out, unlocked the kitchen door and went in, and sat her purse on the bar.

She went to the bathroom to take a quick shower before going to bed. She undressed, turned the water on and waited for the temperature to get just right, put on a shower cap and stepped into the shower. The water was warm and soothing. She soaked for about ten minutes, turned the water off and reached for a towel when she thought she heard a noise. She quickly wrapped the towel around her, pitched the shower cap on the vanity and moved slowly into the bedroom. She picked up the baseball bat her boyfriend kept by the bed. She stood in the middle of the room, listening. After three or four minutes she decided she was hearing things, put the bat down, dropped the towel, took a gown from the closet and slipped it on. She went to the kitchen, dug her phone out of her purse and walked into the living room. She sat down on the couch, pulled her legs up under her, ran her fingers through her damp, blonde hair and dialed. After four rings a voice came on the phone.

"Hello."

"Hi, Billy. You said call you when I got in. Sorry if I woke you."

"That's alright, honey. I'll see you tomorrow; should be in around noon. I'll take you to dinner and that movie you wanted to see."

"Sounds good."

"Get some rest. I'll see you tomorrow, sweetheart," he said.

"I will. Goodnight." She tossed the phone on the couch and went to the bedroom. As she walked through the bedroom doorway she felt a sharp pain in her buttocks, it stunned her and she stood motionless for a second or two. A quick dizziness came over her. She looked behind her and saw something in the hand of a blurred, shiny figure moving toward her.

She staggered and fell down. The blurred figure stuck tape over her mouth. She tried to get up but her legs wouldn't work. Everything was out of focus. The room was spinning. The image of some kind of huge animal appeared and was charging her. She tried to scream but no sound came out and the animal went right through her and disappeared. She gasped and her pulse rate skyrocketed. She fought to stay conscious; her body limp and helpless.

The blurred figure jerked her gown off, wrapped something around her wrist, placed her on the bed and tied her in a spread-eagle position on her back.

Her throat began to close, her air supply becoming less and less. Everything was getting dimmer and dimmer. She looked up toward the blurred figure with pleading blue eyes, gulped for one last breath and was gone. Cynthia Ann Freeman was dead.

26

A dozen police cars, ambulances, TV trucks and a company of reporters were in front of Cindy Freeman's condo. She had been murdered with neighbors only a wall away.

A big uniformed cop, one Mecana and Darcie knew, was standing in the door way.

"Hi, Mecana, Detective Connors," the cop said.

"Hi, Scotty," Mecana said. "Do we know how he got in?"

"No forced entry, so we don't know yet," Scotty said.

Mecana nodded. The cop handed Mecana and Darcie latex gloves. "Doc wants everybody to put these on."

Mecana and Darcie slipped on the gloves and walked in. Mecana spotted two FBI men he knew making notes. One was William Sullivan. He was about Mecana's age and size but looked a lot older. He was almost bald, with beady blue eyes and a dimpled chin. Mecana knew him from their days as street cops in Dallas ten years ago. The other guy was younger, bigger and slimmer. A transplanted Yankee from New York, with thick black hair by the name of George Kaminski. He didn't like anybody.

"What're you guys doing here?" Mecana said.

"She was crossing the state line on a federally regulated flight. That makes it federal," Sullivan said.

"What? You are reaching, Sullivan. That's bullshit."

"Take it up with your boss. I'm doing what I'm told," Sullivan said. Sullivan and Kaminski grinned at Mecana and walked away.

"Where do they get off coming on like that?" Darcie asked.

Mecana stared at Darcie for a moment. He had that Yogi feeling again.

"Makes me mad," she said.

"Happens all the time," Mecana replied. "You'd think they would have enough work with terrorists from two wars to worry about without horning in on local cases. I'll talk to the Chief. Let's have a look."

Two men in white coats, wearing gloves with plastic bags and magnifying glasses, were scanning the bedroom for clues; another man dusting for fingerprints. Doctor Seymour was standing in a corner writing something in a notebook.

Mecana and Darcie walked up to the bed to look at Cindy. Dried blood ran in all directions on the bed like a road map. Her lower body was covered in blood. Part of her missing. Smeared bloody footprints tracked from the blood by the bed disappeared at the bedroom door. Her milky-colored eyes had a fixed stare, like she was looking at someone when she died. Darcie stuck her hand over her mouth and ran to the bathroom.

Doctor Seymour noticed Darcie head for the bathroom. "Damn," he said.

Mecana give her a glance and walked over to Doctor Seymour.

"Hope your partner's not throwing up in the sink, contaminating my crime scene."

"Her first time at a homicide, Doc."

Doctor Seymour shook his head.

"How long you think it took him to do this, Doc?"

"Maybe thirty minutes, a little more."

"When?"

"Early this morning."

"Same drug?"

"Looks like it. No gunshots, stab wounds or head trauma. I'll know more when I get her back to the lab. We got footprints. May be the killer. Had something on his feet, though, can't tell if they were size eight or twelve, too smeared."

"I noticed," Mecana said. "Would you call me when the report is ready? We've got some FBI in here. Don't think they're supposed to be."

"Yeah, I saw them. I'll have to give them a report, but I'll make sure you get a head start."

"Thanks, Doc."

Darcie reappeared. "Never seen anything like this," she said.

"Me neither," Mecana replied. "We have some finger-prints and footprints. He may have made some other mis-takes. We'll have a closer look at her when the lab boys get through."

Darcie gave Mecana a sideways look, frown wrinkles appeared on her forehead. She gulped, covered her mouth and headed for the bathroom again.

Mecana noticed a leather-bound notebook lying under the edge of the bed. He moved closer, bent down and flipped the book open with his pen, and turned the pages with it. Her scheduled flights, hair dresser, accountant and several other appointments were listed, and then he saw it: DOCTOR DURANT, FRIDAY, OCTOBER 12, 2 P.M., BIRTH PILLS. He picked up an evidence bag from the nightstand, put the notebook in the bag with his pen, checked to see if anyone was looking and stuck the bag in his coat. He walked over to the bathroom and leaned on the wall next to the door, and waited for Darcie to come out.

Maybe, he thought, just maybe he knew who the killer was. This Jack the Ripper won't get away.

27

Mecana poured a cup of coffee, took a sip and twisted his mouth like he had bit into a lemon.

Darcie was watching. "Now you know why I don't drink the coffee here," she said.

"Man, tastes like burned leaves." Mecana stuck his tongue out and flicked it like a snake.

Chief Verves appeared at his office door. "Mecana, you and Darcie can come in now."

Mecana dumped the cup in the trash and he and Darcie walked in and sat down.

Verves followed them in and sat down. "I just got off the phone with the FBI. They're not going away. We're going to have to deal with the situation the best we can. It's not worth the effort to fight them. The best course of action is to continue to march and try to avoid them as much as possible."

"Chief, you know that's not going to work. They're going to have priority on everything and we're going to be sucking hind tit," Mecana said, then looked at Darcie. "Sorry."

"It's not a problem," she said.

"I don't like it anymore than you do," Verves said, "but the main thing is to catch the killer. If they can do that, more power to them."

"I may have something that will change that," Mecana said. "Didn't want the FBI to get it." Mecana took the notebook out of his coat pocket and laid it on Verve's desk. "Found this at the scene. It's Cindy's appointment book. One of the appointments was with Doctor Dawson Durant a week ago. Forensics matched Durant's prints on the headboard of her bed with a cup I picked up at the hospital when we had him under surveillance. I think we're back to Doctor Durant. There were other prints, but they haven't come up with a match yet."

"You didn't tell me about the notebook," Darcie said.

"You were too busy throwing up."

"That's interesting, Mecana," Verves said, "but I want you to get that notebook to the property room immediately. A good defense attorney would blow us out of the water for tampering with an evidence claim."

"I'll take care of it, boss, but do you think we have a suspect?"

"I think we need to know how Durant's fingerprints got on her bed and what his relationship with her was. You and Darcie go have a talk with him. Get his story before you go off half-cocked. If he doesn't have the right answers, bring him in."

"What about the footprints?" Darcie asked.

"Too smeared," Mecana said. "He probably had his shoes wrapped."

"Is Cindy a local girl?" Verves asked.

"She hasn't been in Dallas very long," Mecana said. "Transferred here last year from Chicago for a promotion."

"I'll have public relations contact her family. Anything else?" Verves asked.

"Just one," Mecana said. "Throw that damn coffee pot out the window and buy a new one, with a different brand of coffee. That's the worst tasting stuff I ever tried to drink. I still got that horrible taste in my mouth."

"You don't get that notebook to property you're going to have a worst taste than that."

"I hear you, Chief. We're going, right, Darcie?"

"Right."

"Oh," Verves said. "Almost forgot. Didn't turn up anything on the drug prescription. No medical people on it that we could find."

"Darcie, I think we better get the book to property then pay the doctor a visit. You watch his hands, I'll block the door. If he makes a run, make sure you don't shoot anybody else. Especially me."

"I may not have worked homicide before but I'm a good cop, Mecana," Darcie said.

"I'm sure you are, but when someone pulls a gun or breaks to run, a lot of people will overreact. Wanted to make sure you didn't," Mecana said.

"You do your job and I'll do mine, Mecana."

"Good enough," he said.

28

A pretty, young black nurse wearing a bright flowered smock was standing inside the nursing station, writing on a chart when Mecana and Darcie arrived. She saw them and smiled.

"Can I help you?" she asked.

"We're looking for Doctor Durant…Nadine," Mecana said, looking at her name tag. "His office said he was at the hospital." Mecana pushed his coat back and showed her his badge.

"One moment please." She walked away and went into a room down the hall.

Doctor Durant came out of the room. He looked more like a TV doctor than a real one, with his athletic physique, curly brown hair, six-foot-plus body and handsome face.

Darcie stuck her thumb in her belt, her Beretta a couple of inches away under her coat.

"You wanted to talk to me?" He said.

"Is there someplace we could talk in private, Doctor?" Mecana asked.

Durant gestured toward a room across the hall and they went in and closed the door.

"I'm Lieutenant Thomas Mecana and this is Detective Darcie Connors of the Dallas Police Department. We need to ask you some questions about a patient of yours, Miss Cindy Freeman."

"I've been expecting you," Durant said. "I saw what happened to her on the news. I recognize you, Mecana, from seeing you here before the fiasco at my grandfather's house. I can confirm she was a patient, that's all. Patient confidentiality."

"Doctor, your fingerprints were on her bed. You want to explain that? Or do we need to get a warrant?"

Durant let out a big sigh and dropped down on the edge of the bed, pushing the stirrups out of the way. "I guess I don't have a choice but to tell you the truth."

Mecana and Darcie looked at each other, their adrenaline rising.

"I made the mistake of going to her condo."

"Why?" Darcie asked.

"She came in for a physical to get a prescription for birth control pills. When I wrote out the prescription, she suggested I come by and test them, as she put it."

"Then what?" Darcie asked.

"I let it pass, but the next day she called and said she was alone and the invitation to test the birth control pills was still open, so I went. I have a weakness for beautiful women."

"What does your wife think about that?" Darcie asked.

"She doesn't know. I would like to keep it that way. She's very socially connected and this would hurt her standing on the social scene, not to mention what she might do to me."

"Where were you last Wednesday night, Doctor?" Darcie said.

"I anticipated that question, too. I checked my schedule; fortunately I was here all night. I had an emergency that required me to be with a patient."

"You have witnesses?" Mecana said.

"Yes, various staff members. I can give you their names if you need them."

The excitement in Mecana and Darcie's eyes dimmed a bit, and Darcie moved her hand away from the Beretta.

"We'll need that," Mecana said. "Linda Belmont was a patient of yours in Houston, right?"

"That's right. It was about her menstrual problems. I treated her for them."

"You were at a seminar in LA when she was found," Mecana said.

"I've already confirmed that with the Houston Police."

"You mean you confirmed you were in LA when they found her? Not when she was murdered?" Mecana said.

"Yes, that's right. They seemed satisfied with my answers."

"Did you ever see her outside of the medical visits, Doctor?" Darcie asked.

"We had lunch on a few occasions."

"According to the Houston Police report, her roommate said you showed up at their apartment the day she was murdered around one in the afternoon; said she had lunch with you."

"I explained that to the police. I thought it would be best to take her to lunch and discuss her medical condition with her in a different environment than the hospital. She was having a false pregnancy. That can be very traumatic for a young woman."

"What happened after that?" Mecana asked.

"Nothing. I left her at the restaurant and went back to the hospital."

"Did she say where she was going that evening," Mecana asked.

"No. I don't know where she went."

"You didn't see her that night?"

"No. I've already covered all this with the Houston Police."

"Yes, you have, doctor," Mecana said. "Do you know Julie Crawford or Barbara Sadler, better known as Kinky?"

"Don't know anyone named Kinky. I do know the Crawford family. Her dad is our lawyer. I've spoken to Julie a couple times at social functions. She wanted to be an actress, that's all I know about her."

"No hanky panky?"

"No. You're barking up the wrong tree, to use one of my father's favorite phrases."

"Do you recall where you were Monday night two weeks ago?" Darcie asked.

"No."

"We'll check it out," Darcie said.

"Cindy is the only one I had any kind of personal relationship with." He stood up, took the stethoscope from around his neck and laid it on a table. "Can we keep this between us?"

"I suppose so," Mecana said. "One last question. You know, or ever hear, Cindy mention a man named DeMax Baker?"

"Not that I recall," Durant said.

"If we have anymore questions we'll let you know," Mecana said.

29

Mecana and Darcie were having lunch at Brogans, discussing their meeting with Durant, when FBI Agents Sullivan and Kaminski came in and walked over to their table.

"Well, Mecana, got to give you one," Sullivan said. "We just had a talk with Doctor Durant. You beat us there. You're not one of his favorite people."

"I'm not trying to win a popularity contest."

"Too bad that weirdo Carter didn't work out for you. Got another suspect, though, and it isn't Durant. I'll let you figure out who it is."

"You're full of shit, Sullivan. If you had another suspect you wouldn't be telling me."

"Her boyfriend and Durant weren't the only ones she was sleeping with. Seems like Miss Cindy got around," Sullivan said.

"You weren't one of them, were you Mecana?" Kaminski laughed.

"How would you like me to kick your Yankee ass, Kaminski?"

"I don't think I have to worry about that."

"Go away," Darcie said. "We're having lunch."

"I bet you take good care of your pretty little partner, Mecana," Kaminski said, smiling.

Darcie's brown eyes took on a viper stare at Kaminski. A forked tongue could be expected to dart out of her mouth. "If he doesn't kick your ass, I will," she said.

"Oh, a real spitfire, aren't you?" Kaminski said, and began to laugh again as they walked away.

"Don't let them get to you, Darcie, that's what they want. Sullivan is trying to plant a seed, get us to spend time coming up with someone they can move in on without doing the legwork. I know him."

A waiter brought two plates of food and sat them on the table.

"Maybe Sullivan isn't that far off," Darcie said. "She either let him in or he had a key. She may have accidentally gotten hooked up with the killer. Someone we don't have a name for. We know the boyfriend didn't do it. He had his key on him. We should have a rundown on her phone soon, maybe that will give us a name."

"Wait," Mecana said. "It just occurred to me we didn't ask Durant how he got in. We just assumed she let him in. One of two things happened: what you said, or she may have given Durant a key. If she did, what happened to that key? Did he use it again when he killed her? Did someone else get the key somehow?"

"You want to call him and check?" Darcie asked.

"No, we'll do it in person. He's less likely to lie. We'll take it from there."

"Okay. I don't know about you but I lost my appetite," Darcie said.

"Yeah, me too. Sullivan has a way of doing that to people."

"Let's get out of here," Darcie said.

30

"What? You two again?" Durant said. "I thought we were done? If I see you again, you better have a warrant."

"Just one more small thing," Mecana said. "Did Cindy Freeman give you a key?"

"Didn't I tell you that?"

"No, you didn't. Where is it?"

"I think I gave it back to her."

"But you don't know for sure?" Darcie asked.

"No, not something I gave any thought too."

"Doctor, it's important that you remember," Mecana said.

"You think the murderer may have gotten the key, right, and it's my fault?"

"Possibly. We need to know what happened to the key. Call me when you remember." Mecana handed him a card. "Good day, Doctor."

They made their way to the Silverado and climbed in.

"He knows what happened to the key," Darcie said. "Two-to-one it turned up missing, that's why he doesn't want to tell us - afraid we will try to connect him as an accessory."

"If Durant doesn't call by tomorrow morning we'll try a little blackmail. It's obvious he's afraid his wife will find out about his infidelities; we'll threaten to tell her."

"You're vicious, Mecana. I love it. Makes me feel better to know another cheating man is going to suffer. You a cheating man, Mecana?"

"No, my mistress was my work. I didn't have my priorities right. Your ex must have been a fool to cheat on you."

"Why, Lieutenant Mecana, you do have a sensitive side." Darcie smiled at Mecana. "You sound like you still have feelings for your wife."

"I do, we have two beautiful daughters that will always bind us together no matter what we do. I know we both have to get on with our lives. I don't have any fantasies about a reconciliation. We're both past that."

"At least something good came out of your marriage. Mine was quite different. It was a physical attraction that burned out pretty quick for both of us. He started sleeping around; I buried myself in my studies. That was the end of it. College kids that thought they were in love. We weren't."

"We'll, I still think he was crazy for letting you get away."

Darcie gave Mecana a long look.

"What?" Mecana asked.

"Why don't you drive me home and we can discuss this 'til morning."

"I'm not very good at reading between the lines Darcie. Are you saying what I think your saying?"

"You could say that."

Mecana fired up the Silverado.

31

Darcie shook Mecana's arm and his eyes popped open.

"Coffee's ready, big guy." Darcie handed him a cup. "You can drink this."

Mecana rose up in bed, and took the coffee cup.

"It wouldn't have to be very good to be better than that tree bark Verves calls coffee."

"I can fix breakfast, or we can go out."

"Coffee's enough for me."

"Okay, I'm going to take a shower and get dressed. Maybe Durant's memory has improved."

"Sounds like a plan to me. Where's my pants?"

"On the floor where you left them."

The nurse they spoke to before met them in the hall.

"The doctor's not here."

"Where is he, Nadine?"

"Don't know, he hasn't showed up for his rounds. You're here about the Freeman girl that was murdered, aren't you?"

"You know about Doctor Durant and Miss Freeman?" Darcie asked.

"I overheard him and Miss Freeman talking, she was coming on to him something furious. He gets a lot of that from his patients. Some twice his age."

"Do you know anything about a key she gave him?"

"I saw it on his desk in the examining room after she left. I picked it up to take to the lost and found office. He saw me and took the key from me."

"You ever see it again?" Mecana asked.

"No. I was going to throw it away if I did."

"You have any idea where Doctor Durant is?" Darcie asked.

"Maybe his home. His wife is having a big party to-night."

"Why don't you call him? Don't say anything about us, just where he is. We'll wait." Mecana smiled at the nurse. She smiled back.

"Alright give me a couple of minutes. I have to take medication to a patient."

Mecana nodded, and watched Nadine's perfectly rounded derriere move back and forth as she walked away. Darcie scolded Mecana with her eyes and he gave her a sheepish grin.

Nadine returned shortly. "I paged him, called his house and his wife's cell; no answer. Don't know where they are."

"Give us the phone numbers, we'll find him," Mecana said.

"Is that legal, giving you someone's private phone numbers?" Nadine asked.

"It's okay. If you don't give them to us we can get them from the phone company."

Nadine nodded, wrote the numbers on a pad and handed them to Darcie.

Mecana and Darcie left the office.

"What do you think, Darcie, could Nadine be another Durant bed partner?"

"Speaking of bed partners," Darcie said, punching the elevator button, "think we should cool it for a while. Think it over…partner."

"Was thinking the same thing…partner," Mecana said.

PART THREE

32

Darcie was working on Cindy's phone calls at the phone company. Mecana was briefing Chief Verves in his office on the key and Durant's absence when a tall, beautiful blonde came in and walked over to one of the detectives.

Mecana recognized her as Mrs. Durant from the stake-out. She was dressed to the hilt in a green designer outfit that matched her eyes. The dress hugged her slim, curvy body like it was happy to be there. The jewelry she wore could have made a down payment on the national debt.

The detective stood up, said something to her and pointed to Verve's office.

Mecana looked at Verves. "That's Durant's wife, I'll see what she wants."

Verves took a look and nodded. Mecana walked out of Verve's office toward Mrs. Durant. She saw him coming, and struck a pose.

"You Detective Mecana?" she asked.

"Yes, I am."

"I'm Lisa Lamont Durant," she said, and looked at Mecana like he was supposed to applaud.

"Would you like to sit down, Mrs. Durant?" Mecana slid an office chair close to her. She looked at the worn, soiled chair and frowned. "No, thank you. I'll stand."

"What can I do for you, Mrs. Durant?"

"My husband had nothing to do with the murders of those young women, and yet you insist on interfering in our life and harassing him. Thought I would make one last attempt in person before we sue you and the city. Leave my husband alone, Mr. Mecana."

"Mrs. Durant, your husband has, or knows the location of, evidence we need. I'm trying to conduct a murder investigation. When he produces the evidence I'll go away. You know where he is?"

"He's at home, helping me prepare for my party. What evidence do you think he has, Mr. Mecana?"

"I'll take that up with him."

"You can discuss it with me."

"I don't think so."

"Mr. Mecana, my husband has one of the most successful practices in the country. The wealthiest women in Dallas come to him. That translates into a lot of money. More in one year than you will probably make in a lifetime. You're hurting his practice, costing us money by showing up at the hospital. That has to stop."

"Mrs. Durant, you have your priorities, I have mine. If money had anything to do with it, I wouldn't have come to work this morning. You tell your husband he can come see me, or I will meet him somewhere if he doesn't want me coming to his workplace. He has my number. He knows what I want. Now if you will excuse me, I have work to do."

"It's apparent you do not understand the seriousness of your dilemma, Mr. Mecana. I want to see your supervisor."

"That's him in the office," Mecana pointed at the glass panels. "His name is Robert Verves. He's Chief of Homicide. I'll introduce you."

She brushed her long blonde hair away from her neck, gave Mecana a snobbish glare, and followed him to Verve's office.

"This is Mrs. Durant, Chief. She wants to talk to you. She's not happy with the way I'm conducting the Freeman investigation."

"Have a seat, Mrs. Durant," Verves said.

She eyed the chair before being seated.

"What can we do for you?"

"Your detective Mecana insists on harassing my husband. Dawson has told him all he knows about Miss Freeman. She was a patient, that's it. As for the others, he knows nothing about what happened to them. Leave us alone."

"Mrs. Durant, I can appreciate your concern. I know sometimes it appears like we don't exercise the best protocol, I apologize for that. But we're trying to solve some brutal murders. We have to make sure we cover all the bases."

Mecana stood in the doorway behind Mrs. Durant.

"Would you like some coffee, Mrs. Durant?" Verves asked.

"No, nothing, Mr. Verves. I came here to give you the opportunity to avoid a lawsuit. Mr. Mecana is a public servant who has overstepped his authority. I want him taken off the case, now. If you don't, you both may be out of a job." She stood up and Verves followed.

"I can't do that, Mrs. Durant, sorry."

She batted her long eyelashes. "Mr. Verves, you will regret your decision. I know the Mayor personally," she said before stalking out.

When she was out of ear range, Verves eyed Mecana. "You better find that son of a bitch or we'll know the Mayor personally, too," Verves said.

"I will."

"What do you know about the Durants and the Lamonts, Mecana?"

Mecana reached in his inside coat pocket and pulled out a notebook.

"She has an interesting and controversial family, the typical poor little rich girl. Her father is Doctor J. Barnard Lamont, a heart surgeon in Houston, very rich. The mansion the Durants are living in has been in her family for over a hundred years. Her great-grandfather Jackson Bernard Lamont inherited a railroad from his father, got in some trouble embezzling money from the company and fled from Austin to London. The charges were dropped two years later; he returned, moved to Dallas, married a socialite and built her that mansion. They had a son. She turned up missing when the boy was four, and was never found. Her family raised the boy, who became even richer during the Industrial Revolution and World War Two before her father inherited it all.

"Lisa's sister, Shelly, two years older, died from an accidental fall when they were teenagers. Her parents couldn't get it together after that and divorced two years later. Her mother remarried and lives in Florida. Dawson Durant's family are average working people. There are two other boys. One in the Army in Iraq and one is a teacher in California at a small private school. She met Durant at Baylor. She has a genius IQ over 160, works as a freelance professional photographer for all the top magazines. Durant's kind of the male version of the trophy wife.

"That's about it."

"You do your homework, Mecana," Verves said.

"She's not going to leave us alone, Chief. Her kind thinks rules don't apply to them. I've seen it too many times," Mecana said.

"I think you're right about that," Verves said. "Her lawyer paid me a visit asking for your head. Said he was going to pursue legal means to have you removed from the case."

"That doesn't surprise me," Mecana said. "I expected her to get her lawyer on me."

"I'll stick with you as long as I can," Verves said, "but you have to crack this case or both of us may be looking for a job."

"I will. It's just a matter of time," Mecana said.

"We may not have a lot of that," Verves picked up his empty coffee cup. "Bring me some good news, Mecana."

Mecana nodded and left.

33

Dawson Durant adjusted his black bow tie and took Lisa's arm as they entered the ballroom. The magnificent room was big as a basketball court. The social elite of Dallas were waltzing on the mirror-shined marble floors to the music of a large live orchestra. Lisa had invited everyone who was anyone. The expensive crimson gown she wore complemented her beauty.

"You better behave yourself, Dawson," Lisa said. "Don't embarrass me in front of my friends."

"I didn't want to come to this damn thing anyway. I should have been at the hospital instead of helping you push the servants to get this place ready for tonight."

"You think spending a day with me is a waste?"

"Don't twist my words. You know what I mean."

"You're not a country bumpkin anymore, Dawson, you have an obligation when you're class."

"What, kissing each other's ass?"

Lisa saw the mayor coming toward them. "We will discuss this later."

The mayor looked suave in his black tuxedo. Not a gray hair out of place. He was a good-looking man, though not in Dawson Durant's league. He shook hands with Dawson and kissed Lisa's hand.

"Everything is perfect, Lisa," he said. "There's something I've wanted to discuss with you. I need a new chairman for my reelection campaign. Why don't you stop by the office next week?"

"Thank you, Mayor Pratt, I would like that," she said. "I have something I want to discuss with you, too."

"You're quiet tonight, Dawson," the Mayor said.

"Kind of tired, been a long day," he said and smiled.

The Mayor smiled. "Have to circulate," he said and walked away.

"You really want to help that jerk get reelected?" Dawson asked.

"Yes, it would be fun. He may not want me if we don't get Mecana off your back. I had a talk with him, but it didn't do any good. I'll drop a word on the Mayor when we have our meeting."

"I can handle my own problems, Lisa."

"It doesn't look like it, my dear," she said.

"I need a drink," Dawson said.

"By all means, enjoy yourself, sweetheart," Lisa said sarcastically.

Dawson looked bewildered as he walked to the bar.

The president of the social register came up to Lisa and they made small talk while Doctor Durant worked on a gin and tonic.

It wasn't long until an attractive brunette caught his eye.

34

The next morning, Mecana was on his way to the phone company when his phone rang.

"Mecana, my wife said she came to see you. Did you tell her about Cindy?"

"No, I didn't. I told her you had evidence I needed."

"I don't know what happened to the key. I really don't. I remember dropping it back in my pocket when I unlocked

Cindy's door that night and it disappeared some time after that."

"Finding that key may find a killer, Doctor. I hope it's not you. May have to go to your wife, see if she can help your memory."

"No, don't do that. Lisa said she was going to the Mayor to get you fired. I'll see if I can talk her out of it."

"Doctor Durant, if the Mayor wants my job he can have it. I don't intend to back off one bit doing what I think will find a killer."

"She's a determined woman. When she sets out to get something she usually does."

"Me too. Do you have a personal relationship with Nadine?"

"She's my nurse."

"That wasn't what I asked you. I'll make it simple: Are you fucking her?"

"I don't have to answer that."

"You just did. Don't leave town, Doctor, you're still on my shit list. I'll be in touch." Mecana hung up and pulled into a parking space at the phone company.

Darcie met him at the door. "Didn't find much, but I do have the transcripts." Darcie picked up the paper and begin running her finger across it.

"She called her boyfriend several times in the last two weeks. She made a call to the pizza place almost everyday and the pizza place called her twice. She must really like pizza. Two calls to Durant's office. All the other calls were to businesses, no individual names. That's as far as I've got."

"Any of those calls to a medical facility, besides Durant?"

"No."

"What was the name of the pizza place?

Darcie flipped a page. "Lets see. Big Top Pizza."

"Well I'll be damned. DeMax."

"What's a DeMax?" Darcie asked.

"Not a what, a who. A boyfriend of Kinky Sadler. De-Max Baker. Street name 'Stitch.' We checked him out before you came aboard. A real character. He thinks of himself as a ladies' man. Him and Durant have a lot in common. I wonder if there's anything that went on besides delivering pizzas. Let's go have a talk with him. He may know something we need to know. I'll drive."

Darcie followed Mecana to his truck. They got in and drove away.

"Did you find Durant?" Darcie asked.

"He kind of found me. His wife came by the office. She's trying to get me fired and Durant doesn't know what happened to the key. I 'm not sure I believe him."

"Have they got any kids?" Darcie asked.

"Didn't see any on the report. If they do I feel sorry for them."

"What about the nurse?"

"He didn't say he was screwing her, but he might as well have. If we solve the Freeman murder it will solve all the others. I'm convinced of that. Durant is at the top of my list."

"I don't know about Durant, but I agree it's one killer," Darcie said.

"Glad you agree, partner," Mecana smiled and winked at Darcie.

Mecana made a turn on South Freemont Street, a block from DeMax's.

The big Harley wasn't in the driveway. Mecana pulled in the drive and cut the engine.

"Looks like DeMax isn't here. I'll check to make sure. You can stay in the truck."

Mecana walked up to the door and knocked several times - no answer.

An old black woman, with a rake comb stuck in her hair and wearing a faded, flowered house coat and flip flops appeared on her porch at the house next door. "If ya lookin' for DeMax, mister, he ain't there. Bunch of men with 'FBI' on their shirts showed up this mornin' in droves, hauled 'em way."

"You know why?"

"Don't know, rough with the boy. Slammed 'em to the ground. One of 'em sit on his back. Put cuffs on him. No need, boy wasn't tryin' to resist."

"I see. They take his Harley?"

The old lady nodded. "Don't get know respect," she said, shook her head and went back in her house.

Mecana opened the truck door and got in.

"You hear that?" he asked.

"Yeah, I heard. They must think he's the killer."

"Maybe so. If it had been for something else the locals would have showed up."

"What now, Sherlock?"

"Don't know exactly. Hell, I wouldn't think DeMax could peel an apple, let alone perform precise surgery."

"I wonder if they're questioning him without a lawyer present," Darcie said.

"Let's go find out," Mecana replied.

35

Mecana and Darcie stepped off the elevator in the federal building and walked down the hall toward Sullivan's office. A small, square wooden box extended a couple of feet out into the hall beside a drinking fountain.

"That one?" Darcie asked, touching the box as they walked by.

"Yep, don't see why they don't take that damn thing out. It's like they think it's going to come back, and they can put a 'Coloreds Only' sign over it again."

Mecana knocked on a door with 'Special Agent William E. Sullivan – FBI' painted on it. A voice from the other side said, "Come in." Sullivan was seated behind his desk, holding a file. A picture of his hero, J. Edger Hoover, hung on the wall behind him.

"Well, well, Mecana. I figured you'd show up." Sullivan dropped the folder on his desk, leaned back in his chair and propped his feet up on the desk. "We got him."

"You got who?" Mecana asked.

"The mutilator, of course. Was right under your nose and you couldn't see him."

"You talking about DeMax Baker?"

"You do know."

"DeMax is a petty crook but he's not a killer, especially this kind," Mecana said.

"That's where you're wrong, Mecana. He knew all the victims, his alibis are shaky. We found underwear of two of the victims in his house. We'll have a confession before the day's over."

"What about Houston?"

"We're still working on that one. Maybe where he got the idea."

"You think he will confess to murdering three women?"

"Yep. When we get through with him."

"You going to take a rubber hose to him?" Mecana asked.

"Look, Mecana, I don't have to take that shit from you. We're going to charge him with the murders. Did you know he's a former Army medic? His street name is Stitch because he stitches up the wounded in the neighborhood."

"Don't you think we've checked him out, and everyone else that remotely knew any of the victims?" Mecana said. "The only name that keeps making me nervous is Doctor Dawson Durant."

"Mecana, take your lady friend and get out of my office."

"Where's DeMax?" Darcie said.

"He's in interrogation. Going to take him to your jail after he gives us a confession."

"I want to see him," Darcie said.

"I don't think so," Sullivan said.

"Does he have a lawyer?"

"No, you want to get him one?"

"No, I am one. He's entitled to have an attorney present during questioning. Let us see him."

"We've done everything by the book, Missy."

"My name is Attorney Darcie Connors, or Detective Darcie Connors, not Missy. Take your pick, Mr. Sullivan. You understand?"

Sullivan's eyes took on a squinted stare at Darcie. He got up and slid his chair back. "Leave your guns on the desk and follow me. I'll take you to him, Counselor."

Mecana looked at Sullivan and grinned. They followed Sullivan down the hall to a room. Sullivan unlocked the door and they all went in.

Kaminski was sitting on one side of a long metal table and DeMax on the other, in handcuffs; a yellow notepad and pen lying in front of him. Kaminski turned to see who had entered.

"What the hell are those two doing here, Bill?" Kaminski asked.

"She's a lawyer."

"No shit?" DeMax said, looking at Darcie.

"That's right," Darcie said. "Now if you two will let us talk to the accused in private."

"Can't do that," Sullivan said.

"If you don't, you're violating his civil rights," Darcie replied.

"You can watch him through the window," Mecana said, and pointed to a big mirror on the wall.

DeMax leaned forward and looked at the mirror. "I'll be damned," he said.

"You got fifteen minutes," Sullivan said, as he and Kaminski walked out and closed the door.

DeMax looked at Mecana. "You put the feds on me, man?"

"No. You play ball with us and we may be able to get you out of here."

"Like what? Don't know who did it. Feds said I did. Tellin' me how I carved up all them pretty ladies. Make me want to throw up. Know'd them all, but didn't do nothin' but fuck 'em."

"Watch your mouth, DeMax," Mecana said. "Thought you didn't know Julie Crawford?"

"Didn't know her name 'til they showed me a picture. Seen her at Griffin's. Played a little paddy cake with her in the back room one time, that's all."

"What about Cindy Freeman?"

"Liked to fuck. Called me when she wanted a good one."

"What did I tell you about your mouth?" Mecana said.

DeMax cut his eyes up at Darcie. "Sorry, lady."

Darcie nodded.

"DeMax, if you were visiting Cindy that much how come your prints didn't show up?"

"Guess 'cause I kind of got in the habit of wearing gloves and wiping things down, you know, since you cops are always trying to take my black ass to jail."

"You're saying you deliberately removed your prints from her place? You know how incriminating that looks? You fucked up, DeMax," Mecana said.

DeMax looked at Darcie again. "He got a bad mouth, too."

"He sure does," Darcie said, and flashed her big brown eyes at Mecana.

"Sorry, lady," Mecana grinned.

"Didn't hurt any of them ladies," DeMax said.

"We believe you," Mecana said, "but if there's anything you haven't told us, now's the time."

"Can't think of nothin' else. Everything's kind of mixed up in my head."

"Did you know Cindy was seeing a Doctor Durant, DeMax?" Darcie asked.

"Yeah, she says she fuckin' that pussy doctor, too. No never mind to me. She a nympho, or something, anyway, wore me out."

"What about her boyfriend? You know him?" Darcie asked.

"No. She always calls me when he's gone on a trip."

The door opened and Sullivan and Kaminski walked in.

"Times up, Councilor," Sullivan said.

"If you're going to charge him you better have more than circumstantial evidence, Sullivan," Darcie said.

"We got witnesses that saw him at the Freeman girl's place the day she was murdered. He just admitted he removed his prints from her place. Why would he do that if he didn't have anything to hide?"

"That was supposed to be privileged information, Mr. Sullivan. I'll make sure you never get it into court," Darcie said.

"We won't need it. I'll have a confession when I get through," Kaminski said.

"Don't sign anything, DeMax," Darcie said. "I'll see if I can get you a lawyer."

DeMax nodded, raised his cuffed hands and pushed the pen and notepad further back on the table.

Darcie and Mecana walked out. A group of reporters were waiting in the lobby when Darcie and Mecana got off the elevator.

"Hey, Mecana!" one yelled. "We hear the FBI has got the mutilator."

"You better ask them about that. We don't think they have the right man."

A young woman with 'KXTU TV' printed on her shirt, fire red hair and big breasts stuck a microphone in Mecana's face. "You sure it's not just sour grapes, Mr. Mecana, because you didn't catch him?"

"I don't have anything else to say," Mecana said, speeding up his walk. They pushed their way through the reporters outside to the Silverado.

36

At eight the next morning, Mecana was on his way to pick up Darcie when Rustin Kemp called.

"Rustin, how you doing, boy?"

"Getting ready to go home. Working on getting my shit together. How about you?"

"Ah, you know, chasing my tail, trying to solve this case."

"I saw on the news the FBI arrested DeMax. Don't seem like he would do that."

"He didn't. They're looking for a scapegoat. Won't last long, though, when the real killer strikes again."

"Yeah, what I figured. I've decided to let you have it. Just wanted to say thanks for everything. Know you'll catch him. Hope it's before he kills someone else."

"Me too. What're you going to do?"

"Got some GI Bill left. Think I'll be a lawyer with my wife's help."

"Good choice. I'm sure you will make a good one."

"Hope so. Catch that son of a bitch, Mecana."

"I will."

"There's something stuck in my head about the night I was stabbed. I can't get a handle on it yet. I know it's important, though. A lot of things I didn't remember about that night are starting to come back to me. Maybe I'll remember what it is later. I'll let you know if I do."

"Good, I can use all the help I can get."

"Watch your back, Mecana."

"You bet."

Mecana pulled into Darcie's driveway, cut the engine, got out and walked up to the door and rang the bell. The door opened and Darcie handed him a cup of coffee with one hand and ran a brush through her shiny black hair with the other.

"Have a seat and drink some coffee, I'll be ready in a few minutes. First time I've seen you in a suit. Like the red tie. You clean up good."

"So do you," he said.

Mecana sat down, took a sip of coffee and Darcie disappeared into the bedroom.

He got up and walked into the bedroom to the open bathroom door, took a drink of coffee and watched Darcie as she looked into the bathroom mirror applying her lipstick. Mecana couldn't take his eyes off her. That little black dress fit perfectly.

"You're a beautiful woman, Darcie."

Darcie looked at Mecana's reflection in the mirror and smiled. "Somebody got up horny this morning."

"Well you shouldn't look so damn good."

"Thanks. I think."

"Maybe I better change the subject," Mecana said. "We need to go or we're going to be late for the nine o'clock news conference to play nice with the FBI."

"Do we have to go?"

"Yeah. I'm walking on thin ice with the powers-that-be as it is."

"I'm ready, let's do it."

"That's not a good choice of words, Darcie."

"Mecana, I think the old adage is true."

"What's that?"

"A woman is looking for a relationship when she has sex; a man is just looking for a place." She smiled, walked by Mecana, flipped his red tie with her long red fingernail and kept walking toward the door.

37

A group of reporters was camped outside the District Attorney's office, yelling questions at anyone who went in or out of the office. When they saw Mecana, they converged on him like bees on pollen.

"What's happening, Mecana?" a young reporter asked. "You still think they got the wrong guy?"

"The District Attorney will have a statement shortly."

"That wasn't what I asked you. Answer my question."

"No comment," Mecana said.

"Is it true you're going to resign, Mecana?" she asked.

"No comment," he repeated.

"What about you, lady, you got a comment?" She thrust the microphone toward Darcie.

"Miss, you best move away and let us through before I put that microphone in a most unusual place."

The TV reporter stared at Darcie for a moment before backing off.

A little bald-headed man, holding his recorder in front of Mecana spoke up. "Have they arraigned Mr. Baker yet, Mecana?"

"Not that I know of. The District Attorney and FBI will have a statement for you. I've got nothing else to say."

Mecana and Darcie walked past a recently-installed podium in front of the District Attorney's office and went inside. The office was filled with lawyers and police, including Chief Orr.

The District Attorney was talking to FBI Agent Bill Sullivan. "We don't have a strong case here, Bill. You better come up with some more evidence or we can't get an indictment."

"Don't worry, Mr. Seville, we will," Sullivan said.

Randall Seville had been the District Attorney for almost ten years. He was a neat, well-dressed, average sized forty-something man with short gray hair. The latest gossip was he was going to run for the U.S. Senate next year. That might not be possible if the Baker case blew up. His star was hitched to a shaky wagon.

Chief Orr saw Mecana and walked over to him. "Looks like I don't have to worry about paying anymore bills, Mecana."

"I don't think you worry about anything anyway, Orr, except when your next meal is. Freeloaders like you get on my nerves."

"That was a shitty thing to say, Mecana. Fuck you," Orr said and walked away.

"Not in the best of moods, are we?" Darcie said to Mecana.

"He wouldn't make a pimple on a policeman's ass," Mecana said.

Chief Verves spotted Mecana and Darcie. "Glad to see you decided to wear a suit, Mecana, and join the rest of us. Darcie, you always look good."

"Thanks, Chief," she said.

"I expect you two to be on your best behavior. I know you don't agree with this but we have to let it play out."

"Chief, you know there's a rush to judgment here to convict somebody because it's a high-profile case," Mecana said. "It's easier when the suspect is a poor black man."

"Don't try to put me on a guilt trip, Mecana. I don't see you coming up with anything. I stuck my neck out a mile long to protect you and you're not giving me anything. I can't do it anymore. If you don't like what's happening, resign."

Frown wrinkles appeared on Mecana's forehead, he looked at Darcie. His steel gray eyes sending a message. She shook her head no. "Can we go now?" he asked.

"Yeah, get the hell out and keep your mouth shut."

Darcie took a step closer to Verves. "Just so you know, Chief, I agree with Mecana."

"Get him out of here, Darcie," Verves said.

Mecana and Darcie made their way back to the elevator.

"You had me worried for a minute there, partner," Darcie said. "I thought you were going to clock him."

"I was close. Verves is afraid of losing his job. He will have his twenty next year and still has a kid in college."

"It's understandable he's a little jittery with all the pressure on him," Darcie said.

"Maybe so, but you know as well as I do that DeMax didn't murder anyone, but he may be convicted on circumstantial evidence because they want a conviction so bad." The elevator doors opened and Mecana and Darcie got on.

38

Mecana whizzed along the highway on his way home, thinking of all the people he had spoken to and investigated. Only one kept turning up as a possible suspect, Doctor Dawson Durant, and he had some iron clad alibis. He was either missing something or he was way off base and his mind wouldn't let him turn loose of his one and only suspect. Rustin had given up, maybe it was time for him to do the same; go visit his daughters and figure out where his life was going from here.

He pulled into his driveway and cut off the Silverado. The guy next door, who he hadn't had a conversation with in five years, was watering his lawn. Mecana had quit doing yard work when his wife left. A lawn service handled it now. The inside of the house wasn't much different. He had a maid come in three days a week. He probably could have made out better if he moved to an apartment, but somehow he just couldn't let go of the house. It was nothing fancy, like most of the three bedroom bricks in the neighborhood, but it was special to him. Maybe subconsciously it was a way of holding on to a little piece of his family.

The first thing he always did when he got in the house was check his answering machine. He had pictures of his kids by the machine to look at when he talked to them. They had his gray eyes and their mother's Southern Belle beauty.

The message light was blinking. He punched the play button, and grabbed a beer out of the fridge.

"Daddy," the voice said. It was his oldest, Emily. "I know you probably won't get this until tonight so call me on my cell phone. I didn't want to bother you at work. I have to fix my car. The man at the garage said I needed new brakes."

Mecana grinned. She was using psychology to ask for money.

Mecana dialed his daughter's number.

"Hi, Daddy. You get my message?"

"Yes, I got it. How much is it going to cost?"

"Two hundred and fifty, I think."

"Doesn't your mother ever give you any money? I send her the biggest part of my paycheck."

"She said you bought it, you have to keep it up."

"That's your mother's revenge for me buying a sixteen-year-old a car."

"Are you going to give me the money, Daddy?"

"Have the garage pick it up. I don't want you driving it if the brakes are bad. Tell them to call me and I'll give them my credit card number."

"Oh thank you, Daddy, you're the greatest!"

"Naturally. Where's Morgan?"

"She's at dance practice."

"She doing okay?"

"Yes. She's a pest, though, always wanting to go with me."

"That's what little sisters do. You take care of her."

"Yes, Daddy. Thanks for fixing my car. Maybe I can come see you before long."

"That would be nice. I love you, baby. Tell Morgan I love her, too."

"I will. I got to go, Daddy."

"Bye, sweetheart."

"Bye, Daddy."

Mecana sat holding the phone after Emily hung up, his mind working overtime again. He picked up her picture and sighed. "I love you baby," he said and sat the picture down.

The doorbell rang. He hung up the phone and moved to the door and looked through the peep hole. It was Darcie, wearing jeans, a pullover red sweater and holding a sack.

He opened the door and Darcie stepped inside and gave him a big smile.

"After the ordeal today, I figured you needed some company tonight," she said. "I brought an old friend in case we need a little help." She held up a bottle of Jim Beam and smiled again.

"Might be a good time to get reacquainted. I'll get the glasses," Mecana said.

39

It was a Saturday and Mecana and Darcie slept in. Later, Darcie was fixing breakfast and Mecana was watching the news when a bulletin came on, saying that DeMax Baker had confessed to being the mutilator and was giving the FBI the details of his gruesome crimes.

"Holy shit! Come here, Darcie. Look at this."

Darcie came into the room, wearing nothing except one of Mecana's dress shirts that barely covered the essentials, and sat down beside him on the couch.

"What the hell is DeMax doing?" Darcie said. "Why would he do that? He's not the mutilator!"

"Do you know if they have appointed him a public defender, Darcie?"

"I can make a call and find out. He damn sure needs one."

"Can you do it?"

"No, they won't let me. His attorney will have to come from the attorney pool. Whoever is up next."

"That's a piss poor way of doing it."

"Actually, it's a pretty good way to keep the system balanced."

"Maybe. Get dressed, let's go find out if he's lost his mind."

"What about breakfast? I was fixing you pancakes."

"I'll take you to McDonalds."

"Always the big spender. Let me cut the stove off and find my undies and jeans."

The short, obese jailer had a loaded key ring in his hand. He shook his head at Mecana. "I can't do it, Mecana. Unless you have something to do with his defense, I can't let you talk to him. I've got strict orders, no visitors. That means cops, too."

FBI Agent Bill Sullivan appeared in the hallway right on cue, walking toward Mecana and Darcie. "What're you two doing here?" he asked.

"Checking on that rubber hose," Mecana said. "What's this bullshit about a confession, Sullivan?"

"He decided to tell us about the Freeman murder after we found his prints in her condo and he couldn't account for his whereabouts that night."

"What did you do, have him sign a confession you typed up after he signed it?"

"He read it."

"Sullivan, you know damn well that man is not the mutilator. The only drugs he knows about are the ones you buy on the streets."

"Why do you keep taking up for this guy, Mecana? What the hell is he to you?"

"He's someone that's being used to further yours and the District Attorney's careers. You don't give a damn if he's innocent or guilty as long as you get a conviction."

"Has an attorney been assigned to him, Mr. Sullivan?" Darcie asked.

"One you know, Detective Connors. A Nicklaus Booker."

"Know him, Darcie?" Mecana asked.

"He's my ex. A lousy husband, but a good lawyer."

"You never said anything about him being in Dallas."

"You never asked. Before you ask the next question, I had the court restore my maiden name."

"Mecana, you're wasting your time. Based on his confession, the judge has refused to set bail and until someone overrules that, no visitors."

"Looks like we will have to have a talk with your ex."

"Looks that way," Darcie replied.

"Why don't you do that, Mecana, and leave my prisoner alone," Sullivan said.

"I'll call Nick," Darcie said.

"Let's go," Mecana said. "Something smells in here and it has a suit on."

"Mecana, you can't be right all the time," Sullivan said. "Did you ever stop to consider that?"

"Not where you're concerned, Sullivan. You don't give a shit about anyone but yourself."

"You're damn right. I learned a long time ago you have to take care of number one first," Sullivan said.

"Let's go, Darcie, I got a bone to pick with you, too."

"Didn't know, did you, Mecana?" Sullivan laughed.

Mecana didn't say anything and walked away.

"Why the hell are you mad at me?" Darcie asked, looking surprised.

40

Mecana was silent as he drove back to his place. For some reason he felt Darcie should have told him about her ex practicing law in Dallas. He was a bit confused over his feelings because he and Darcie were only sometime lovers. There weren't any commitments. She didn't owe him any explanations and he didn't her.

"You want to stay over for the weekend, Darcie?"

"I don't think so. I don't know if I cheered you up but I did me. Think I'll go work out and drive down to Waco to see my family. We can check in with Nick on Monday."

"Why do I have that used feeling?" Mecana said, never taking his eyes off the road.

"Maybe you were, but you got your share."

"You don't pull any punches, do you, lady?"

"Nope. Kind of a waste of time. I care about you, Mecana, but I don't want this to get out of hand. You seem to be a little jealous over Nick. That puzzles me a bit. I don't want to complicate my life. I like who I am and I like who you are. Let's keep it that way."

"Fine with me. Just drop in anytime you want to get laid and I'll take care of you."

"Now you're getting nasty. Time for me to go home."

Mecana pulled into his driveway and cut the engine.

Darcie got out and closed the door. "I'll see you Monday and we'll go have a talk with Nick. Try to get some rest. I may be back." She smiled and walked away.

Mecana couldn't help but smile, too. She had a way of putting everything into the proper perspective.

Mecana watched Darcie drive away and went in the house and turned on the TV to watch a football game, but couldn't get his mind on it. He kept thinking of Darcie and realized he was beginning to think about her too much. She had made it quite clear she was happy with the way things were.

He spotted the almost-full bottle of Jim Bean on the kitchen table. He walked over to the kitchen cabinet, got a big drinking glass and poured the liquor to the rim, put the glass to his lips and began to let the whiskey slide slowly down his throat. He blinked his eyes and continued swallowing the whisky. By the time the glass was empty he didn't care what Darcie thought, and by the time the bottle was empty he didn't care what he thought, either.

He fell asleep with the TV on, the empty whiskey bottle lying on his leg.

41

Mecana's head felt big as a watermelon as he stumbled to the bathroom the next morning. He had never tied one on like that, not even in the Marine Corps, and hadn't had a drink of anything in over a year.

He called Darcie and her phone kept ringing. Finally he heard her say, "Hello."

"I was beginning to wonder if your phone was working," he said.

"I just woke up. You made me feel guilty. I didn't go to Waco. I took a bottle of Jim Beam to bed with me and we got drunk, or at least I did. Did you know he doesn't care how you feel?"

"Sounds like you're still drunk."

"I may be."

"Fix some coffee and I'll be by to pick you up and we'll have a talk with your ex."

"If my legs work, I'll do that," Darcie said.

Mecana was going to have the last laugh. He wasn't about to tell her he did the same damn thing.

When he rang the doorbell she opened the door holding a water bottle on her head.

"Come in. You can help me get ready for my funeral."

"Damn, you're not kidding. You look like forty miles of bad road."

"Oh, shut up. The coffee should be ready, pour me a cup. I'll see if I can navigate to the bathroom and wash my face."

Mecana brought her coffee to the bathroom. She was bent over the sink washing her face, her panty-covered butt sticking out. She looked in the mirror and saw him staring at her rear end.

"Don't let it even cross your mind, Mecana."

He grinned, handed her the cup and walked back into the living room.

It was after ten when they arrived at Nick Booker's office. He had a plush office in one of the ritzy office buildings. His matronly secretary informed them it would be a few minutes, that Mr. Booker was finishing up with a client on the phone.

Mecana and Darcie sat like zombies, still reeling from the night before. After almost an hour, Booker came out of his office, Mecana and Darcie half asleep. He was tall, good-looking with bright blue eyes and neat brown hair, dressed in a gray suit.

He walked over to Darcie to embrace her. When she didn't respond he changed his mind and shook hands with her. "How are you, Darcie?"

"Doing okay, Nick. This is my partner, Thomas Mecana. We wanted to talk to you about DeMax Baker. We think they have the wrong man." Mecana shook hands with him.

"Come in and we'll talk." He led them into his office and gestured for them to sit down; he sat down behind his big mahogany desk. What looked like a good reproduction of a Picasso hung on the wall behind him. A picture of a beautiful young blonde on the desk caught Mecana's and Darcie's eyes. They glanced at each other for recognition. The new woman in his life.

"I was assigned the case a couple days ago," he said. "Was hoping I wouldn't have to do anymore public defender work. Haven't had time to review it. Looks like it's an open and shut case with his confession. Maybe I can cut a deal, save his life."

"Mr. Booker, he's not the killer," Mecana said. "He's being railroaded by overzealous FBI agents and prosecutors."

"Like I said, I haven't had a hard look at it yet, but it looks like he's saying he did do it, Mr. Mecana."

"I'm sure his confession was under duress, not of his own free will."

"That's a serious charge. I would watch who I threw that out to."

"Nick," Darcie said. "We have a suspect we think is the killer. What we need you to do is get a postponement or a change of venue to give us time to get the evidence we need to arrest the real killer. Don't let this go to trial anytime soon."

"I'm not sure what grounds I would have to do that. As you know, Darcie, this conversation could be construed as tampering by the court."

"I told Mecana you were a good lawyer. Don't make me take it back."

Booker looked at Darcie and his eyes softened. "I'll see what I can do."

"Good. We're counting on you."

"Thank you, Mr. Booker," Mecana said.

"Call me Nick. Your name's Thomas, right?"

"That's right, but everyone calls me Mecana, kind of rolls off the tongue better. If I ever need a lawyer I'll give you a call."

"Good. You do that. Darcie, why don't I give you a call? Take you to lunch."

Darcie gave Mecana a quick look and Booker picked up on it.

"Maybe I should take both of you to lunch," he added.

Darcie ignored the comment. "Thanks for your help, Nick."

"My pleasure," he said.

PART FOUR

42

Doctor Durant came out of his office, handed a patient a prescription and saw his wife sitting in the waiting room.

"What are you doing here, Lisa? Is something wrong?"

"We need to talk."

"As you can see, I have patients. Can't this wait until I get home?"

"No, it can't," she said and rushed past him into his office.

"Nadine, I'll be out in a minute," he said.

"Yes sir."

He followed Lisa into the office and closed the door.

"Okay, what's so damn important that you have to scare the hell out of my patients?" he asked.

"I want you to take a vacation. Get out of town for a while, until this murder investigation is over."

"Mecana doesn't have any proof of anything," he said.

"They arrested a black man for the crimes, but until they put him on trial I think you should go away."

"I can't just walk off and leave my practice."

"I would have agreed before, but now that flatfoot won't back off. Go visit your brother, play golf."

"Don't you think it would look more suspicious if I suddenly left my practice and disappeared somewhere?"

"That's what I want you to do, disappear. I'll handle the police and press. Mecana's not going along with arresting the black man. He'll have him back on the street by tomorrow. He's after you. If you're not here he will quit snooping around."

"You mean he will quit annoying you?"

"Yes, that's part of it," she replied.

"I have to get back to my patients," Dawson said.

"You know I know best, Dawson," she said.

"Not always, Lisa. You just think you do."

"I want you to fire that prissy black nurse, too. I don't like the way she looks at you."

"Go home, Lisa. Let me get back to my patients."

"Dawson, please do what I ask before Mecana puts you in jail."

"I'll think about it."

43

When Nadine finished filing paperwork, she locked the office door and walked down the long hallway to the parking garage. It had been a long day. She was getting tired of it. Durant didn't give a shit about her anyway. She was just a convenient piece of ass when he was bored.

There were only two other cars on the third level, and no one but her in the parking lot. She punched her key lock and the lights came on in her car. She had an eerie feeling someone was watching and turned around.

There stood a person wearing a plastic suit from head to toe. The plastic figure lunged at her with a syringe. She swung her purse at the syringe, knocked it to the ground and it smashed into a thousand pieces. She jumped back, screamed and began to run, dropped her purse and picked up speed as she headed for the stairs.

She could hear footsteps behind her. She grabbed her phone from her jacket pocket and tried to dial 911, but was too scared and dropped the phone. When she got to the stairs she took a quick look over her shoulder and the plastic figure was gone. She took a couple of steps down the stairs and looked back again; no one was there.

She ran inside the building and saw one of the security guards coming at her, waving a .38 pistol. He looked to be in his mid-sixties and was shaking almost as much as she was.

"Was that you screaming, Miss?"

"Yes, someone was after me!"

"Where did they go?"

"Don't know. He was wearing a plastic suit, trying to inject me with something! I broke the syringe and took off running."

"You stay here, I'm going to go look."

"No, don't leave me! Call the police. Tell them to call Detective Mecana. He knows me. My name's Nadine," she said, pointing at her name tag. "Thanks for coming to my rescue."

"What I'm here for," he said, holstering his pistol. He liked the flattery and gave her that Barney Fife twisted-mouth look.

"The police. You need to call 911," Nadine said, pointing at the phone on his belt. "He may still be in the building."

"Oh yes, of course." He grabbed his phone and dialed.

A voice on the phone said, "Emergency 911."

"This is security guard Willie Black, license number 42671 at the Liberty Office Complex on 34th street. We have had an assault. At the moment we don't know where the suspect is. The victim is okay. She's with me. She knows a Detective Mecana and has requested you notify him. Her name is Nadine."

The dispatcher's voice came on the phone again. "A unit is on its way. I'll notify Mecana."

"Thanks, we will be waiting in the downstairs lobby," he said and hung up.

44

The police were already at the scene when Mecana and Darcie arrived. Sergeant Wayne Overfield, an athletic-looking thirty-eight-year shift supervisor met Mecana and Darcie at the door. "Whoever it was is not in this office building now. We covered every floor," he said. "I haven't interviewed the victim yet, thought I would let you do that. I recovered her purse and phone. We're still looking for evidence."

"Good. There should be some cameras. Check them out and let me know if we got anything."

"I'll check," Overfield said.

Mecana walked over to where Nadine was sitting. She had calmed down some and was drinking a cup of coffee.

"How you doing, Nadine?" Mecana asked.

"Better. Whoever that was scared the crap out of me!"

"Tell me about what happened."

"I was walking to my car, alone, when this thing snuck up behind me, trying to inject something in me. He was covered head-to-toe in a plastic suit. I knocked the syringe out of his hand and ran back in the building and he ran away."

"A plastic suit?"

"Yeah, it looked like one of those radiation outfits you see the x-ray people wearing. I couldn't make out the face."

"Did he say anything?"

"Nope, just lunged at me with the needle and I took off."

"Did you hear or see him leave? What kind of car?"

"No I was too busy running. There were two cars in the parking lot when I came out but I didn't pay much attention to them. I think one was a red sedan and the other one was a black SUV. I didn't notice what kind, both were new looking."

"Was there anything else you noticed about him - how tall, fat, slim, anything?"

"He was taller than me, average size maybe."

"How much taller?" Mecana asked.

"I don't know for sure, just taller. I was so scared I don't remember."

A police officer walked up to Mecana carrying a plastic evidence bag with the pieces of the busted syringe. Some of the liquid contents were still inside the syringe pieces.

"What do you want me to do with this, Mecana?" he asked.

"Give it to me, I'll take it to the lab later. Nadine, it might be a good idea for you to spend the night at a hotel. I'll send a female officer to keep you company and we'll talk in the morning."

Nadine took another drink of coffee and tossed the cup in the trashcan. "I'm ready. I need to get away from here."

"I'll stay with her, Mecana," Darcie said. "Maybe she will remember more later."

"That's a good idea if you're up to it. I'll stick around here and make sure we go over this place with a fine tooth comb. The killer is getting careless; broke his MO. Taking chances. He may have left something for us."

"I'll see you tomorrow," Darcie said. "Let's go put you to bed, Nadine."

Darcie and Nadine walked out the remote doors of the lobby.

45

Mecana called Darcie the next morning at the hotel. "Nadine wants to leave town, Mecana, she's scared," Darcie said.

"I can understand that but we need her for a witness. I hope she will do it voluntarily. The parking lot video should show us something. They're supposed to have it here by one. See if she will come to the police station to view it with us. She may be able to add something."

"Hold on a minute." Mecana waited. "She said okay, but wants police protection until she leaves town."

"Tell her she's got it. See you at one o'clock."

"Okay," Darcie said.

Mecana and Verves were as nervous as a whore in church, waiting for the techs to set up the video. Darcie and Nadine showed up and they all sat down to take a look.

A flash of light hit the screen then went out. All that was visible were two shadowy figures too dim to make out. The film rolled and jumped as the events Nadine described took place in the dark.

"Damn, damn, damn!" Mecana said, jumping to his feet. "What kind of mess is this? I thought we were supposed to be in the electronic age. Don't those people ever check their cameras?"

"I'll have the techs take a look," Verves said. "They can do amazing things. Maybe they can enhance it to make out the details."

"Yeah do that, Chief. This has been the most difficult case I ever had. You would think we could catch a break, son of a bitch."

"Well," Nadine said, "you can see enough to know I didn't make it up. That madman is after me for some reason."

Mecana flopped down in his chair again and let out a big sigh. "Yes, I can see that much. But the man in that tape is so vague it could be Mickey Mouse for all we know. I thought we had something we could throw at Durant this time."

"Why do you keep connecting Durant?" Darcie asked. "Maybe he doesn't have anything to do with the murders. He has some good alibis. They check out."

"My gut tells me there's a hole in those alibis somewhere. I just have to find it."

"What if your gut's wrong and you're after an innocent man?"

"It's not."

"Well, I'm as disappointed as you are, Mecana," Verves said, "but after fifteen years I've learned you're right more times than you're wrong. Pick Durant up for questioning. We'll improve this video some and show it to him; he just might break."

"I tried to call him before I left work to remind him he was scheduled at the hospital for surgery tomorrow," Nadine said. "No answer from any of his phones. He does that sometimes, even his wife won't know where he is. I know I'm damn sure not going back there."

"We'll pay him a visit at that hotel he lives in. His wife can call the Mayor," Mecana said.

"I'm sorry I was so rough on you about Baker, Mecana," Verves said. "To tell you the truth, that's what I thought, too. I was trying too hard to be politically correct."

"Get Nadine a body guard for us, Chief," Mecana said. "You coming, Darcie?"

"You're my partner," she said and picked up her purse.

46

Mecana turned on to the long drive and drove up to the front of the 18th century mansion. Tall stone pillars and big hundred-year-old double front doors marked its elegance.

"You ever been in a house this big, Mecana?"

"Not unless you count the American Airlines Center."

Two Hispanic-looking men with hedge cutters were trimming hedges nearby. Mecana rapped on the door with the door knocker three times before the door opened. A small, middle-aged black-eyed woman wearing a maid uniform stood in the doorway.

"May I help you?" she asked with a strong Spanish accent.

"We're from the Dallas Police," Mecana said, showing her his badge. "We're looking for Doctor Durant."

"Mister Durant not here."

"How about his wife? May we speak with her?" Mecana asked, stepping into the doorway.

"No, no, not come in," she said. Mecana pushed past her and she ran into another room.

Lisa Durant appeared a moment later wearing a white bikini; the top barely covering her large breasts and the bottoms hanging on her shapely hips. She had a towel wrapped around her shoulders, water dripping to the floor.

The little woman returned with two helpers with mops. "I try to stop them," the woman said, as the two other women mopped up the water as fast as it hit the floor.

Lisa spoke to the woman in Spanish. ("It's okay, Maria, I will take care of it.")

"Sí," she replied, and they continued to mop up the water.

"I was informed you were leaving the police department immediately, Mecana," Lisa said.

"Don't believe everything you hear."

"What do you want?" she asked.

"We're looking for your husband. We have some questions to ask him."

"You can talk to our lawyer. He's not answering anymore questions."

"I'm afraid he doesn't have a choice this time. We have a warrant." Mecana pulled the paper out of his coat pocket, took a couple steps closer to her and held the warrant up for her to see. "Where is he?" Mecana asked again.

"He's at the club, playing golf, I think. He always plays on Wednesdays," she said.

"You don't know for sure?"

"No, I had to go out early this morning on a shoot, but I know his schedule. He plays every Wednesday. He wasn't here when I got back."

"When was that?" Mecana asked.

"Around eleven," she replied.

"Where does he play?"

"The Broadview Country Club on J. B. Lamont Road. Now leave me alone," she said, rubbed her wet hair with the towel and walked away.

Mecana stood looking at the shining spiral staircase that climbed to the second floor and disappeared, the giant paintings of the Lamont clan patriarchs, the burgundy velvet drapes and eighteenth-century hand-carved furniture. The huge crystal chandelier in the center of the magnificent room probably cost as mush as Mecana's house, he thought.

Darcie saw Mecana gazing and interrupted. "Seen enough?"

"Yes. How's your golf game?" Mecana asked.

"Never played," Darcie replied.

"I think three times for me, if I remember right."

There were golfers everywhere; it would be hard to find the doctor. Mecana's limited golf experience told him the clubhouse would know when he teed off and who he was playing with.

An elderly man with white hair, wearing knickers and a dark tan was minding the store.

"Excuse me," Mecana said. "What hole would Doctor Durant be on?"

"None. He didn't show. Was scheduled to tee off at eight with whoever was here. He doesn't care who he plays with as long as he plays. Very unusual for him to miss tee time. Golf's his passion. Likes it more than being a doctor, I think."

Darcie looked at Mecana. "What now, Sherlock? You think his wife clued him in?"

"Hell, he could be in that house and it would take a week to go through all the rooms," Mecana said. "I read about this hotel in Vegas in the eighteen hundreds that had a tunnel running from the hotel to a nearby brothel. The married men would sneak off to the brothel and their wives never knew they had left the hotel. Maybe he's got a tunnel."

"Only you would think of something like that, Mecana," Darcie said.

"It's true," Mecana added.

"Maybe we should back off a little, see if he turns up."

"We can't do that. We have to find him before it happens again."

"I agree with the questioning part of what we set out to do, Mecana, but we don't have anything stronger than what they got on DeMax. If you count the confession they have more; Mrs. Durant is not completely wrong. She could get us for false arrest and a lot more."

"The difference is we're after the real killer."

"I hope you're right, but you're so locked in on Durant. It's becoming an obsession. What if you're wrong?"

"I'm not. Let's go put out an All Points Bulletin on him."

"Wish I was as sure as you are."

"You will be."

"I don't know. Has it crossed your mind that the guy on the tape is doing this alone? That he's your everyday, ordinary, run-of-the-mill serial killer, and doesn't even know Durant?"

Mecana gave Darcie a puzzled look. "Remind me to get a new partner," he said.

"Hey, I'm just trying to be helpful," she said.

"Well, you're not."

"Is this a partnership or not?" Darcie said. "I have an opinion once in a while that might just be worth listening to. Take me to my car. I don't think I want to ride with you. There's an apartment I have to go look at, anyway. I've got to move."

"Whatever," Mecana said.

47

Mecana waited in the lounge of the forensics lab while Doctor Seymour went to check on the status of the report on the drug used in Nadine's attack. After about thirty minutes he came out of the lab.

"We ran some comparison tests that we can do in our lab and there is a similarity, but I need a more sophisticated analysis to say for sure. It will take a couple of weeks for that."

"How would he get that much of the drug, Doc?"

"Easy if he's a doctor or someone that had access to it, like a pharmacist, pharmaceutical salesman or even a patient. The drugs would come in a box of six vials if it was the usual amount, and those vials would have three to five hundred units per vial. He would have enough to kill ten more women. A normal dose is ten units and he injected two hundred. The drug could have sat there for years and actually gotten stronger or have been contaminated. Either way, he didn't care."

"We haven't told anyone what drug was used, so it must be our killer," Mecana said. "I'm pretty sure it's the same drug," Seymour said.

"Doctor Durant is the only one I've come up with that fits all the prerequisites. Now we can't find him. He's scared to death of his wife. She's the one with all the money and he doesn't want to lose it. But why mutilate them if your motive is to shut them up? Seems like that's enough. Why the brutal overkill? That's the part that's confusing me. The psycho element. I'm not sure about the attack on Nadine. He could have not intended to kill her, but send a message of some kind."

"Regardless," Seymour said, "I would bet my last dime the guy who tried to kill Nadine murdered all of the others."

"Yeah, this one's kind of got me buffaloed, Doc."

"You'll figure it out, you always do."

"Thanks, Doc."

"Where's your shadow?" Seymour asked.

Mecana grinned. "Don't think she would like that comment too much, Doc. Pretty damn independent."

"Didn't mean any harm."

"I know you didn't. They're going up on her rent and her lease is up next month. She's looking for a new place for the old price."

"In this town, good luck," Doctor Seymour said.

48

The last thing Mecana needed to see when he got home that night was a red Mustang convertible sitting in his drive way, but there it was.

The door was unlocked. He heard the TV blasting when he walked in.

There sat Emily, munching on some stale chips he had opened two days ago.

"What are you doing here? Where's your mother?"

"I came by myself. Your key was where it always is. You should get a new hiding place, Daddy."

"You came by yourself?"

"Yes, I ran away. I'm going to live with you."

"Your mother doesn't know where you are?"

"Don't think so," she said, flipping through the channels.

"Cut the TV off, we need to talk."

Emily turned off the television and stood up and brushed her long brown hair from her face. Mecana stared at her. It had been a year since he last saw her. She wasn't a little girl anymore. He was looking at a full-grown woman.

"Why did you run away?"

"Mom was going to take my car! I told her you bought the car and she had no right to take it."

"Why was she going to take your car?"

"Because I made a 'C' in Algebra and a 'D' in PE."

"How do you make a 'D' in PE? Nobody makes a 'D' in PE. All you have to do is show up!"

"That's why I made a 'D'. I didn't see any reason to go to that class, running around the gym, accomplishing nothing."

"And the Algebra?"

"Who's going to use Algebra? Waste of time."

"I see. You have become an expert on life at sixteen."

"No, but it's my car. Not hers!"

"Have a seat and let me call your mother."

Mecana dialed. "Hello? That you, Tom?"

"Emily is here," Mecana said.

"Thank god! I was about to call the police. I've been worried sick."

"She's fine, Amanda. She said you were going to take her car."

"She's been ignoring her studies ever since you bought her that car. All she wants to do is run up and down the road with her friends."

"She told me. Don't you think that might be a little drastic?"

"Don't you have any sense of responsibility, Tom? You don't have to deal with the everyday situations. You can stand back and play the hero without having to make the hard choices."

"You're right, Amanda. It's your call. If you think that's the thing to do to get her back on track that's what you should do."

Emily was listening. "I'm not going back," she said.

"Go sit down, young lady. I'll deal with you in a minute," Mecana said.

Emily folded her arms, frowned and marched back to the couch and sat down.

"I'm up to my butt in alligators, Amanda. You're going to have to come get her."

"You always are. Nothing is more important to you than your job."

"Let's don't get into that now. Forget what I said, I'll drive her home and catch a flight back to Dallas. It will give me a chance to see Morgan."

"Tom, you need to make her understand that she keeps the car only if she brings her grades up and starts showing a little more respect."

"I'll talk to her. I'm going to leave now. I have to be back in Dallas tomorrow."

"I'll be expecting you."

"Bye, Amanda."

Emily jumped up from the couch and ran over to Mecana. "Don't make me go back, Daddy, I don't want to!"

"Emily, you can't stay here. I have no one to take care of you."

"I can take care of myself. I'm a big girl now."

"Yes, you are, but you still need someone around to keep everything going. I don't know when I'll be home. I work all hours. You wouldn't like it here. All your friends are in Austin and your mother is trying to do what's right for your future. She loves you very much. The same as I do."

"Is she going to take my car?"

"Probably for a little while, but get your grades up and she will give it back. Tell you what I'll do, you go home and behave yourself, and next year when you graduate, I'll buy you a new car - if you graduate with at least a 'B' average."

"A new car?"

"Yes, a new one."

"A convertible?"

"Yes, deal?"

"Okay, deal," she said and hugged his neck.

"Just one thing. Don't say anything to your mother about the new car. That will be our little secret."

"Okay," she said.

"Let's get you back to Austin. I have to work tomorrow."

"I can drive myself. I came up here by myself."

"I know, and the thought of that scares me to death. Let me make a phone call and we'll go."

Mecana punched his speed dial and Darcie answered.

"Your nickel, Mecana," Darcie said.

"My sixteen-year-old daughter showed up unexpectedly in the car I bought her. I have to drive her back to Austin. I'll catch a flight and be back tomorrow."

"What happened?" Darcie asked.

"Oh, growing pains. Trying to assert her independence. But I got it handled. I bribed her."

"You're a real diplomat, Mecana."

"I thought so. I'll call you when I get back. You can pick me up."

"Okay. I'll petition the court for the search warrants in the morning."

"Good. See you tomorrow," he hung up the phone. "You need to go to the bathroom before we go, Emily"

"I'm not five years old anymore, Daddy. But I am hungry, let's stop at McDonalds and get a hamburger."

"You got it kid. Like old times."

49

Darcie called headquarters and had them send two uniforms to Durant's Liberty Building Office to pick up his computers for analysis. When she got there it was open, and Lisa Durant was going through her husband's desk. Lisa turned to look when Darcie walked in, closing the desk drawer hurriedly.

"Mrs. Durant, you will have to leave the office. I have a search warrant and no one can take anything out of this office except the police."

"May I see the warrant please?" Lisa asked. Darcie took the warrant from her purse and handed it to Lisa. She glanced over it and handed it back to her.

"What do you expect to find, Detective Connors?"

"Don't know yet. What are you looking for?"

"Making sure he didn't leave a check book or any credit cards. Someone could rip us off big time."

"You know where your husband is?"

"No, I'm as much in the dark as you are. Filed a missing persons report. Haven't heard from him."

"Mrs. Durant, we will find your husband. Don't help him. If you know where he is you should let us know, or you will be charged with harboring a fugitive."

Her eyes got big and she stared at Darcie like she was from another planet. "Has it occurred to you, Miss Connors, that something may have happened to Dawson? Why do you think I filed the report? Your bunch is making all kinds of wild assumptions and harassing me instead of finding Dawson."

"We have an APB out on him. Every police station in the entire country is aware we're looking for him."

"I have to go," she said, picked up her pearl-inlaid purse, and hurried away.

Two young uniform cops walked up to the open door; one still trying to follow Lisa's backside down the hall with his eyes.

"Alright, guys, come in, show's over. I need you to package everything that's not nailed down. Make sure you don't damage anything, then lock up and take everything to the office. Put the keys in my desk drawer."

The officers nodded. Darcie walked out the door. Her phone rang. "You on the ground, Mecana?"

"Yeah, Love Field. I'll be waiting for you on taxi row."

"I'm not too far away. I'll be there in about fifteen minutes."

"Thanks, I'll be watching for you."

Mecana spotted Darcie's black Charger and stepped onto the curb. She stopped and he got in.

Darcie made a turn off the exit and they headed downtown.

"Get your daughter back on the right path?"

"I hope so. Big mistake buying that car, it's caused me all kinds of problems."

"Kind of glad I don't have any."

"What, cars?"

"No, kids. Smart ass."

Mecana grinned.

"Lisa Durant was at the doctor's office looking for something when I got there," Darcie said. "She said she was looking for credit cards. I think she was looking for something else. I had all the office stuff sent downtown. I don't think we're going to find anything. I'm sure she's already anticipated the search warrant for the house. You know she hates your guts. Blames you for all her problems."

"Most likely. Take me by the house, I need to shower and get my truck," Mecana said.

"You have a problem with lady drivers?"

"You want the truth or a lie?"

"Never mind. I got another apartment to look at anyway. On the other side of town but the rent's good."

"Is it safe?"

"Got a fence and security guards like the old place, but I haven't had a chance to check out the neighbors yet."

"Alright, I'll pick you up after lunch and we'll pay a visit to the Durant Mansion."

"One-thirty, my place," Darcie said.

"I'll be there," he said.

50

Mecana stepped out of the shower and his telephone rang. It was his youngest, Morgan.

"Daddy, did you tell Emily you were going to buy her a car for graduation?"

So much for secrets, Mecana thought. "Yes I did, if she made good grades and behaved herself."

"What about me? I graduate from junior high next year. Are you going to buy me a car, too?"

"Don't think so. We'll figure something out."

"It's not fair! I make good grades and I'm not going to get anything."

"I didn't say that. How about a trip to Disney World?"

"Will you go too?"

"We'll see."

"Daddy, mom wants to talk to you."

Mecana sighed and considered hanging up. "Put her on, Morgan."

"Tom, how am I going to teach these kids work ethic and responsibility when you spoil them like that?"

"Christ, Amanda, I love my kids. I'm trying to be a good father."

"Instead of buying a car, help me with her college tuition," she said.

"Amanda, you're a CPA, you make more money than I do. I send you most of my check. Why don't you tell that good-for-nothing boyfriend of yours to get off his ass and pay his own way?"

"That's none of your business, Tom. I can see this conversation is going nowhere. We'll discuss it later."

"Much later, as far as I'm concerned. Put my daughter back on the phone so I can say goodbye."

"Yes Daddy?"

"Morgan. You plan on me and you going to Disney World next spring."

"Thanks Daddy!"

"Tell Emily she's going to get the car I promised, because I promised."

"Yes, Daddy, I'll tell her."

"Bye, baby," he said.

51

Mecana was still thinking about his kids when he picked up Darcie. "Darcie, you may be right."

"Right about what?"

"Not having any kids. I love mine to death but being a parent is a hard job. Even harder when you have to do it long distance."

"Something else happen?"

"My thirteen year old thinks she's not getting her share."

"Is she?"

"She is now, got me to promise I would take her to Disney World. I may have to sell the house to pay for all I promised them."

"That's not your kids' fault."

"No it's not. You call Booker about DeMax?"

"He got the judge to set bail since there is some question of his guilt with the attack on Nadine. They released him this morning."

"Good. I bet Sullivan is fit to be tied."

"That man gives me the willies," Darcie said.

"Not exactly my favorite person, either. He's been trying to get me fired ever since I testified against him in an Internal Affairs investigation when we worked together on the Dallas PD. Had a drug dealer tell me he paid Sullivan off, so I told the investigating team. Unfortunately, the guy turned up dead before he testified and the charges were dropped. Sullivan resigned and a couple years later turned up wearing an FBI badge."

"We don't find Durant soon he might get his wish," Darcie said.

Mecana and Darcie arrived at the Durant mansion early, parked where they could see the entrance and waited to approach Lisa on neutral ground.

She came out about an hour after they got there and headed downtown in her Lexus, parked and went in a camera shop on Whitehurst.

Mecana and Darcie did the same. They walked up beside her as she was making a purchase.

"Fancy meeting you here, Mrs. Durant," Mecana said. "Did you know your husband was not at the golf course? Do you have any other suggestions?"

"I don't have anything to say to you, Mecana; or your whore."

"Well, she's not a whore, but if she was, your womanizing husband would pay big bucks for her."

"Mecana, what the hell did you just say?" Darcie asked. "You're comparing me to a whore."

"Sorry about that, Miss Connors," Lisa said. "Mecana seems to bring out the worst in me."

"He has a way of doing that," Darcie said, frowning at Mecana.

"I would think you would want to cooperate, Mrs. Durant," Mecana said.

"Are you trying to match wits with me, Mecana?"

"I wouldn't dare. Where is he?" Mecana asked.

"I don't know."

"You expect me to believe that?"

"Since you are a crude imbecile that chooses to do this in public, let's get it over with once and for all. My husband and I have been having marital difficulties, primarily for the reasons you implied, which are none of your business. Yet you continue to harass us about those brutal crimes with no evidence. You're a worn-out old cop that has lost his edge and you're grasping at straws to save your job. I don't know where Dawson is. My concern now is for myself and I will not answer anymore questions about him. Any other communication you have with me will have to go through my attorney. Leave me alone and go play cops and robbers with someone else."

She snatched up her bag and walked out of the shop.

"I think I have just been told off big time," Mecana said.

"He'd pay big bucks..." Darcie said. "Why the hell did you say something like that, Mecana?"

"Thought she would get mad, lose her cool and spill the beans."

"Well she didn't." Darcie's brown eyes were dancing as she hurried out the door.

Mecana looked at the clerk and shrugged his shoulders. The clerk gave him one back. Mecana shook his head and walked out.

52

Darcie was still sulking when they got back to headquarters. Mecana opened the office door for her, offered to get her a Coke and even complimented her on her pretty green blouse to no avail; nothing worked.

"Okay," he said, "you want me to say it. I screwed up. I'm sorry. You happy?"

"You should be. Insinuating I could be a whore."

"I didn't mean it like that."

Mecana started to pour a cup of coffee, remembered the last time and sat the cup back down.

Darcie was watching. "Contrary to what Lisa said you're not as dumb as you look."

"I eventually get it," Mecana said. Verves walked out of his office.

"You wanted to see us, Chief?" Mecana asked.

"Let me get a cup of coffee first." Verves walked over to the coffee pot, poured a cup of coffee and took a sip. "Okay, let's talk."

Mecana and Darcie shook their heads and followed him into his office.

"As you guys know, the shit rolls downhill. Things have changed again. I have been instructed to take you off the case if I want to keep my job. The boss and District Attorney want to get a fresh face, someone that's not so locked in on one suspect. Plus they're still looking at Baker."

"You agree with that, Chief?" Darcie asked.

"No, but I don't have a choice. I have been told to replace you and that's what I'm doing."

"When is this supposed to happen?" Darcie asked.

"Immediately," Verves said.

"We can solve this case if you don't pull the rug out from under us," Mecana said. "We're getting close. I can feel it in my bones."

"It's not my decision, Mecana. I have to answer to my bosses, too. The Mayor wants you to resign. I'm the only one standing between you and unemployment. Maybe it's because we're both Marines, or you talked me into believing you knew what the hell you were doing, but you keep coming up zero. The public is clamoring for heads to roll and the first one is going to be yours."

"Chief, you yourself said Mecana was right a lot more times than he was wrong," Darcie said. "I know it's frustrating. We're frustrated, too. I don't know about Mecana's bones but like he said, I know we're getting close. Something is going to break soon. The glass is half full, Chief. Give us a little more time."

Verves put his hand on his chin like 'The Thinker' and stared at Darcie.

Mecana kept quiet. He knew she had him. How could any man resist a face like that?

"Alright, Darcie, you convinced me," Verves said. "Give me something positive I can show the boss before I have to do what I don't want to do. It has to be soon." He got up, picked up his coffee cup and headed for the coffee pot, then stopped and looked back over his shoulder and smiled at Mecana. "I think you owe her ten, Marine. She saved your ass."

"Yeah, sure," Mecana said.

"Well…" Darcie said, raising her chin up in an aristocratic pose.

"Well, what? You can't be serious?" She batted her eyelashes. "You are serious. You're still ticked off." He let out a deep sigh, rolled up his sleeves and got down on the floor and did ten one-arm push ups and got up.

"Okay, you satisfied?" he said.

"I'm impressed. Now do it with the other hand."

"Let's go, Simon Léger," Mecana said.

Verves came walking back in the office with his coffee cup filled to the brim, stopped and took a big drink.

Mecana did a little wet dog shake and frowned. "How can you drink that stuff?"

"I like coffee," Verves said looking at his cup.

Darcie and Mecana looked at each other. "Won't do any good to say anything," Darcie said to Mecana.

"Yeah, you're right. It's an acquired taste."

Darcie nodded.

Verves stood there staring at them with a puzzled look.

"Thanks, Chief," Darcie said. "You won't regret this. See you later."

"Yeah, later," Mecana said as they walked away.

Verves sat back down in his chair gingerly, like he had hemorrhoids, sipped his bad coffee and looked out the window. "I already do," he said to himself. "It sure looks lonely out there."

53

Mecana was waiting in the hallway while Darcie went to the little girls' room. A slender, gray-haired man with stooped shoulders and dressed in a dark blue suit walked up beside him. Mecana glanced his way.

"Mr. Mecana, my name is Charles Durant," he said. "I recognized you from TV. I was on my way to see you."

"Yes, sir. We spoke on the phone a couple of times. I'm sorry I had to send someone to search your house. Your son is a wanted man."

"That's not why I came."

"You know where he is?"

"No. I believe something terrible has happened to my son. It's not like him to just disappear."

"I'm sorry, I disagree with you, sir. There's every reason in the world for him to disappear. He's wanted for questioning in the murder of four young women."

"Mr. Mecana, we buried his grandfather this morning. I never told my father about the trouble Dawson was in. It would have broken his heart. They had a special bond. That's why Dawson moved to Dallas. His wife wanted to move into the old mansion, and that gave him the excuse he needed to come to Dallas to watch over his grandpa. He liked women too much, but murder? Never."

"Mr. Durant, I know how you must feel but I don't know what to say to you. Sometimes the people we love the most are the ones that hurt us the most. Your son may not be who you think he is."

"My son has his faults but it's not in him to do those kinds of things to another human being. When he was ten years old he saw two teenage boys on a bridge putting kittens in a sack to throw in the river. He grabbed the sack and ran as fast as he could to get away. The boys caught up to him and beat him to a pulp, but he never let go of the sack. No, he wouldn't, and couldn't, do that. I wanted you to know my boy is innocent. You're wrong about him, Mr. Mecana." Tears began to roll down his face. He brushed them away with the back of his hand and walked away.

Mecana stood there with a lump in his throat.

Darcie came out of the restroom and saw the man walk away from Mecana.

"Who was that?" Darcie asked.

"Doctor Durant's father. He had to get something off his chest."

"He knows where his son is?"

"No. He was coping with the situation the best way he knew how."

"Can't help feeling sorry for him, however this turns out," Darcie said.

"Yeah, you can tell he's a good man; tried to raise his kids right. I've seen it a hundred times. Some turn out wrong no matter what kind of home they come from."

54

Mecana drove away from headquarters thinking about what Charles Durant said. What if he was wrong? He was locked in on the wrong person.

"Awful quiet, Mecana," Darcie said. "You planning your next move or thinking about unemployment?"

"Both, what about you?"

"I can go back to being a lawyer. What would you do if you weren't a cop?"

"Don't know. Too damn old to go back to the Marines. Maybe pull an Orr, and find me a small town that needs a cop and doesn't care too much about his past."

"You know I was blowing smoke with Verves," Darcie said. "I don't have a clue where Durant is, but I trust you."

"Thanks. I hope I deserve it. Let's go get some lunch."

Mecana pulled in to the Brogans parking lot and they went in and found a table. They had just finished their meal when Sullivan walked in.

"Ignore him, maybe he will go away," Darcie said.

"No, Sullivan likes to goad people when he thinks he's got the upper hand. I'm sure he knows DeMax is out of jail."

Sullivan walked past Mecana and Darcie looking straight ahead, like he didn't see them, stopped and backed up to their table.

"Well, I'll be, walked right past my old buddy, Mecana. You're going to be looking for a new job soon, buddy."

"I wouldn't count on it, Sullivan. Didn't you hear about the attack on Doctor Durant's nurse? A guy with the same drug tried to kill her. Don't that sound like the real killer to you? Why do you think they let DeMax out of jail?"

"Mistake, but I'll get him back," Sullivan said. "He's the real killer. That was some copycat. Your boy is dead meat." He paused, looked at Mecana and laughed. "Hey, I made a funny; dead meat."

"There's nothing remotely funny about you, Sullivan. Why don't you move on?"

"Your days are numbered, Mecana. The Dallas Police Department will soon be telling you to hit the road."

"We'll see," Mecana said.

Sullivan laughed again and walked away.

"I don't know why you waste time talking to him, Mecana," Darcie said.

"Kind of makes me understand why some animals eat their young," Mecana replied.

Darcie smiled. "I'm not coming here anymore."

Mecana picked up the check and looked at it. "Okay this one's on me, but don't think I'm going to get them all the time just because you're a woman."

"Why, Mr. Mecana, I wouldn't dare make that assumption," she got up, looked down at Mecana, slid her hand gently down the side of his face across his lips and pushed the ticket towards him with the other hand. "You can get the tip, too."

PART FIVE

55

A plastic-covered figure stepped out of the dark next to a camera mounted above a door and sprayed the lens with black spray paint, opened the door with a key, picked up a bag and got on the elevator. The elevator climbed to the ninth floor. The plastic-covered figure got off and walked up the stairs to the tenth floor exit door.

A big burley cop sat outside Apartment 1028, rubbing his eyes. At three in the morning everyone gets sleepy. He didn't notice the elevator down the hall had stopped on the floor below him.

A few minutes later, he thought he heard a door open and got up to look. He walked to the corner of the hall and looked around the corner, nothing. He started to turn back when he noticed the exit door was slightly open and closing.

He took a step toward the door and a shadow appeared on the wall in front of him. He reached for his revolver and a long needle plunged into the back of his neck. He fell against the wall with a slight thump and slid down the floor to his knees, his body leaning against the wall face-first. He took two more breaths. Death was so quick his hand was still wrapped around the handle of his .357 Magnum. He didn't even lose his hat. A gloved hand inserted a key in the apartment door lock, opened the door, went in, and closed the door. Nadine was sprawled out on her king sized bed in the nude, sound asleep. A bottle of sleeping pills was sitting on the bedside end table next to her. With her jet black hair across her shoulders, and her shapely body, she looked like she was in a pose for a Playboy centerfold.

The plastic figure moved beside her bed, bent down and placed a syringe against the nape of her neck. The needle sliding into her smooth skin. Her big brown eyes flew open. She let out a moan as a gloved hand covered her mouth. She tried to move but couldn't. The drug was paralyzing her. Her breath began to come in short gasps as her body fought the deadly fluid. Her eyes darted back and forth then stopped focusing and became a frozen stare, her body limp.

A shiny scalpel appeared in the gloved hand and began to cut into Nadine's lovely body like she was a side of beef. The exacting cuts sliced her vagina from her body and left a mutilated naked corpse that a few minutes ago was a beautiful young woman. The vagina was placed in a black bag and the plastic-covered figure rose from the ghastly deed with the bag, stopped at the front door, took a pair of plastic foot covers and slipped them over bloody feet from Nadine's blood running off the bed. The figure picked up the bag, slowly opened the door and looked out into the hall. No one was there.

The next morning, a young woman on her way to work found the dead cop in the hallway about 6:30 and made the 911 call. Shortly thereafter, an ambulance and a police car showed up.

56

A somber group of police and medical personnel went about their business in the apartment of Nadine Howell. Mecana and Darcie arrived at seven-fifteen and made their way through a large group of media people in the lobby, rode the elevator up to the tenth floor, stopped in the hallway and looked at the fallen cop. Two medics were preparing to put him into a body bag. Mecana looked into the cold dead eyes of the cop. He saw the small trickle of blood on the back of his neck that had run down to his blue collar. "Whatever got him did it quick."

"Yeah, his hand is still on his gun," Darcie said. Mecana pointed at the key in the lock as they entered, Darcie nodded in recognition.

Doctor Seymour and his staff were doing the usual things.

Mecana and Darcie walked over and took a quick look at Nadine.

"He didn't bother to tie her to the bed," Darcie said. "He's becoming so proficient at it; it's like pulling a tooth for him."

"I don't think he had to, looks like she was already out of it," Mecana said, gesturing toward the sleeping pills.

"Yeah, looks like it," Darcie said, eyeing the bottle.

"Darcie, I'll have a chat with the doctor. Why don't you go talk to the super and find out how this place works. What kind of security. See if Nadine had any visitors lately. If she came in with anyone. I'll join you later."

"Okay I can do that. Meet you down stairs," she said.

"Thanks," Mecana said.

Mecana walked over to Doctor Seymour. "What about the cop, Doc?"

"Looks like the drug got him, too. There's a small hole in the back of his neck," Seymour said.

"I saw it. What time did this happen, Doc?"

"Sometime after midnight."

"Anything different this time?"

"We found small amounts of blood on the doorknob, in the elevator and on the stairwell. It's probably the victims'. Looks like he put something on his feet again, the blood tracks stop at the door. He left a calling card this time. A key in the door. We'll check for prints."

"Let me have the key when you get through with it, Doc. I may be able to get some information from it, too. Where it was made, etc."

"Wonder why he left it there?" Seymour asked. "He's too thorough to forget something like that. It must have been deliberate, but why?"

"That's what I was thinking," Mecana said. "Taunting us with it. Sending a message of some kind."

Robert Verves came in and stopped at the bed and looked at Nadine. "If you're through with your work here, cover her up, damn it," he said to no one in particular and moved over to where Mecana and Doctor Seymour were.

"Well, Mecana, what am I going to tell the media and the boss? The Police Chief will have my ass now and I don't blame him. With a little push from you and Darcie we let the one suspect we had out of jail, now this. What do you think about Sullivan's suspect now?"

"Chief, if you choose to use me as the scapegoat, so be it, but I'm not going down without a fight. If you fire me, I will appeal and keep working the case, with or without the department's support. Darcie is just following my lead and there's no reason to include her in this."

"We had him," Verves said. "Get him back in jail and don't give me anymore bullshit about Durant. For all we know he's dead, too. I'll have to give the boss something to take to the Mayor and City Council, and it's going to be your head. I'm assigning someone else to the case and asking you to resign by the end of the month. I hope you do, I don't want to fire you. I'll try to save Darcie's job if I can. You've got two weeks, either way."

"Fine, whatever. Let's keep this conversation to ourselves. No need for Darcie to know." "I can do that," Verves said. "Doc, let me know what you find when you finish your investigation," Mecana said.

Seymour looked at Verves, Verves nodded yes.

"Alright," Seymour said.

Mecana took the elevator down to the lobby. The reporters came rushing over to him.

"Can't say anything right now, guys, the department will have a release for you later," he said, and kept moving toward a sign on a door across the lobby that read 'Superintendant.'

Darcie was talking to a little man with a bald head, faded blue eyes, wearing a white shirt blue tie and kaki pants. He was leaning his butt against his desk, his arms folded across his chest. He looked frightened.

"This is Mr. Mark Colton, Mecana. He's the super. He said Nadine hasn't had any visitors since the office attack and didn't go out very often. She was planning on moving out at the end of the month but, get this, Durant was a regular visitor."

"When was he here last?" Mecana asked Colton.

"Two weeks ago," Colton said.

"You remember it was two weeks?"

"It was the first of the month. The day I always collect the rent."

"How long did he stay?"

"Until the next morning, I think. Didn't see him leave."

"Did he ever bring anyone with him?"

"A young lady one time. The three of them didn't come out of the apartment until the next day. Doctor Durant's a good looking devil, quite the ladies man."

"Yeah, we know," Darcie said. "Could you identify the woman he brought to the apartment?"

"Think so. A very pretty woman with red hair. I heard Doctor Durant call her name as they were going to the elevator. It was most unusual. I didn't think I would forget it, but I can't think of it now. Too shook up."

"Was it Kinky?" Mecana asked.

"That was it," he said.

"Was that the only time he brought any one with him?" Darcie asked.

"As far as I know."

"You have any cameras in this place?" Mecana asked.

"Only at the front door. The tenants don't want them, say it's an invasion of privacy"

"You think you could find some footage of Durant and Kinky coming in or going out?" "Think so," the super said.

"Why don't you do that for us? Include what was on the disc last night. Call me and I'll pick it up."

"Okay, I'll do that."

"Thank you, Mr. Colton, we'll call you if we need to talk again," Mecana said, handing him a card.

"Yes sir," he said, rubbing his hands together like they were dirty.

Mecana and Darcie came out of the office and the reporters converged on them again. The red headed TV reporter in the lead, her cameraman close behind.

"Come on, Mecana, tell us what's going on," she said. "Was it the mutilator? What about Baker?"

"You'll have to talk to Chief Verves when he comes down. I've got nothing to say."

57

Mecana drove along in thought. Durant had lied about Kinky, which means he could have lied about a lot of other things. DeMax told him she was a swinger but he didn't believe him. She was so young and innocent looking. After all these years as a cop he could still be snookered in, especially by a pretty woman. He was pissed off at himself for it.

Darcie broke the silence. "You think Durant lied about Kinky because he didn't want his wife to know, or because he killed her?"

"I was contemplating that. Could be either one, or both."

"Why would he come back and murder Nadine? Why take that kind of chance when there's no need to shut her up now? His wife knows about all his escapades."

"Most serial killers come out of nowhere to do their killing," Mecana said. "Don't know the victims. A one-victim murderer generally knows his or her victim. In this case it appears we have someone who knew all the victims from the get go, which is a total reversal of a serial killers MO, but that is exactly why I believe the killer is Durant. There's something else going on we don't know about that connects them all."

"I hate to bring this up, but you could be wrong," Darcie said.

"You've told me."

"To use a term you men use, why would you throw away your career and marriage for a strange piece of ass?"

"Compulsive obsession. I've seen men with it before, they have to continually prove their masculinity, it becomes an absolute necessity for survival. Being married to a dominate genius like Lisa could make any man go haywire. He's taken it a step further to the macabre, gone off the deep end. Listen to me, I sound like Doctor Wyler."

"You're making good sense."

"He's out there somewhere," Mecana said.

"Whatever you say, Sherlock," Darcie said, arched an eyebrow and smiled.

"You think you're funny?"

"Trying to be."

"Kind of are," Mecana grinned.

"You need to improve your sense of humor, Mecana."

"Don't have time."

58

Mecana was backtracking Durant when he got a call from the airport police. They had seen the bulletin on Durant and found his BMW in parking lot H2C, locked.

"Leave it alone. Don't touch it," Mecana said. "I'm on my way." He hung up and redialed.

"Hi," he said, "this is Mecana. I need you to send a CSI crew out to DFW Airport to dust a car. Parking lot H2C, red BMW. I'll be there by the time you get there. Good, I'll see you there." He hurried to the Silverado.

When he arrived at the parking lot the airport police, wrecker and crime scene crew were waiting.

He pulled up in front of the BMW, shut off the Silverado, reached behind the seat and grabbed a crowbar, walked up to the BMW, stuck the crowbar in the trunk latch and gave out with a heave-ho and the lid popped open. He almost didn't want to look, but there was nothing there but a sample box of Viagra and a spare tire.

"You want to pop the door for us too, Mecana?" one of the lab guys asked.

"Yeah, stand back." Mecana jammed the crowbar in the lock on the door, grabbed the crowbar with both hands, leaned against it and pushed, letting his weight put pressure on the crowbar until the lock busted, and made a shotgun sound as the handle fell off and the door flew open.

"Let me have a quick look inside before you start dusting." Mecana opened the glove box. Nothing but car papers, insurance and service receipts. He ran his hands under the seats, nothing. The service sticker had a date from the day before on it and showed the car had been driven only forty-eight miles since it was serviced. He stuck the papers in his coat. "You can dust it now."

A mousey little fellow pulled on gloves and snapped the wrist bands as he crawled into the car with his equipment. Another fellow was checking the trunk.

"I need those prints as soon as you can get them," Mecana said.

"Doesn't everyone?" the little man said. "Depends on how many prints and if we got them in our database. If we don't, we have to send them to the FBI and it will take a lot longer."

Darcie appeared, walking toward Mecana. Her high heels doing a high-pitched clickity-clack across the concrete floor. "I got your message, what we got?"

"The airport police found Durant's car. He had it serviced yesterday so we know it hasn't been here for more than twenty-four hours. Why would he have his car serviced if he was leaving the next day?"

"I've seen people do stranger things," Darcie said.

"True. I got the name of the service place on the receipt, maybe he let it slip where he was going."

"Or didn't go anywhere and left the car to make us think that was what he was doing," Darcie said.

"Possibly. We need a rundown on the flights, see if his name shows up anywhere. That's going to take a day or two. Let's go have a talk with the auto service shop. See what they have to say."

59

Mecana drove up to the service sign at Super Auto Lube and a young man wearing a blue uniform with 'Sam' on his shirt walked up to the truck window.

"Can I help you sir?" he asked.

"We're from the police department, Sam. My name's Mecana and this is my partner, Darcie. We need some information about one of your customers, a Doctor Dawson Durant." Mecana cut the truck off, stepped out and showed Sam his badge.

"Doctor Durant's a regular customer. Has a red BMW, always gives us a big tip. He was in a couple of days ago, for the usual service."

"Did he say anything about going out of town, or taking a flight somewhere?"

"No. If he was going out of town he always had me take him to the airport and store the car until he came back. He was supposed to come back for tires today; hasn't shown up yet."

"How long have you been servicing the doctor's car?" Mecana asked.

"Since he bought it a couple of years ago."

"If he said he was coming back for something before, did he?"

"Yes, always. He loved that car like some men love a woman."

Darcie glanced at Mecana and grinned.

"What do you mean, Sam?" Mecana asked.

"He had it serviced like clockwork, and we picked it up once a week to wash and polish it. If it didn't sound just right he would bring it in for me to check. He was so afraid someone would hit it, he parked in two parking spaces to keep anyone from getting too close."

"Did he always bring the car in himself?" Mecana asked.

"He didn't trust anyone to drive that car except himself and me. If he couldn't bring it in he would call me and I would pick it up, and then deliver it back to him when we were through. What's this all about? Has something happen to Doctor Durant?"

"We don't know, Sam. That's why were checking. No one has seen him in the last three days."

"That's too bad, he's a nice man."

"You knew him pretty well, didn't you, Sam?" Darcie said.

"Would think so."

"You said he loved that car. Do you think he would leave it in an airport parking garage?"

"Never, he would be too afraid someone would scratch it. No, that's something he wouldn't do."

"Thanks, Sam, you've been very helpful," Mecana said.

"I have to get back to work. Hope nothing's happened to Doctor Durant."

"We do too," Mecana said.

Mecana and Darcie climbed back in the truck, Mecana fired it up.

"You thinking what I'm thinking, Darcie?"

"He didn't drive the car to the airport and he's not on a flight."

"Looks like someone may have punched his ticket," Mecana said. "We're chasing a ghost."

"Could it have been DeMax?" Darcie asked. "He was out of jail."

"The only connection between them is Cindy Freeman. Durant said he didn't know DeMax and DeMax only knew Durant by what Cindy told him"

"Could they have been lying and there was some kind of disagreement, a love triangle, that they didn't own up to?" Darcie said.

"I wouldn't think so. DeMax was there for one thing, and it wasn't for long lasting love."

"Sullivan could be right," Darcie said, "if we tie the two together."

"That's a scary thought," Mecana said.

"Even scarier than that is if it's DeMax. He has a partner."

"You know if Sullivan is right I'll have to move out of Dallas. Couldn't show my face again."

"Then let's hope he's not right. I like being your partner."

60

Lisa leaned forward in her chair and gave Lineal Crawford a cold stare.

"Lineal, I pay you a fortune to take care of my legal affairs and a six figure retainer fee, not to mention the millions my family has already paid you over the years, and you're not doing your job. I want Mecana off the case. He got the black guy out of jail and he's coming after my husband again. You're supposed to have some influence in this town but I haven't seen it."

"They revoked Baker's bail, he will be arrested again," Crawford said. "That should move him away from your husband. The department will assign him to another case and that will be the end of it."

"Mecana has a one track mind. He will pursue Dawson and harass me as long as he has the authority to do so. It doesn't matter what they do with Baker."

"Mecana has been on the Dallas police force for fifteen years, Lisa, it's going to take a little time. The Police Chief promised me he would take care of it, but it has to be done in the right way. Hopefully we can put enough pressure on Mecana that he will resign, if the arrest of Baker doesn't solve our problem."

"I've heard all that before. 'Hopefully' doesn't cut it. If Mecana is not off the force by next week you're fired," Lisa said. "I've got too much invested in Dawson - financially and emotionally - to see it all go down the drain."

"We can sue. Would you like me to do that?"

"I want him gone, Mr. Crawford, you understand? Gone," she said, angrily. "Can you get it done or not?"

"Yes, but like I told you it will take a little time. By the way, where is Dawson? I didn't see him at the golf course Wednesday."

"I convinced him to lay low for a while. Doctor Handan is going to take care of his patients."

"I'll get it handled, Lisa, but you have to understand this is a very emotional time for me, too. My daughter was murdered. Contrary to what some people think, I want justice like everyone else. It just happens to be a coincidence that a suspect was already a client."

"I know. I'm sorry for you, but Mecana is not going to solve the case. He has a vendetta against me and Dawson. He's not looking for the real killer."

"I'll push the Chief. He owes me. I know where all the bodies are buried and he knows it. He can't afford to not do what I want."

"Unless he decides to bury yours," Lisa said.

"He wouldn't dare. I've got proof put away just for this kind of thing. You can count on it. Mecana is good as gone."

Lisa batted her big green eyes and studied Crawford for a moment.

"Alright, Lineal, next week. No more excuses."

"Thank you. Sorry for the inconvenience."

"It's not inconvenient, it's degrading and annoying and I won't stand for it. I always get what I want. You know that."

"I know, Lisa. I know."

61

Mecana pulled into DeMax's driveway. The Harley wasn't there. The old black woman from next door was sweeping her porch. She had on the same housecoat and flip-flops. The only thing different was she didn't have the rake comb in her hair. Mecana walked up to the porch and she stopped sweeping. "Suppose you lookin' for DeMax again," she said.

"That's right. You seen him?"

"Saw 'em yesterday. Put a bag on his bike and left. Ain't been back, far's I know."

"Did he say where he was going?"

"Wouldn't tell if'n he did," she said and started sweeping again.

Mecana stood there looking at her for a second or two; decided she meant what she said. He took a window tour around the house, looking in the windows and went back to the truck. "He was here, but gone now," he told Darcie.

"Think he'll come back?" Darcie asked.

"Don't know. This whole thing gets more bizarre by the minute."

"What now, Sherlock?"

"Don't say that anymore!" Mecana said, and slammed his fist onto the dash of the truck. "It's beginning to really piss me off!"

"Sorry, what the hell, didn't mean to upset you!" Darcie looked at the imprint on the dash. "Won't do it again."

Mecana shook his head back and forth, gritting his teeth. "What am I doing? My fault we're where we are with this. I was so sure. Now, I'm not sure of anything."

"Hey, it's alright. I know how you feel."

"I'm sorry," Mecana said. "Didn't mean to take it out on you. I wasn't going to tell you but Verves plans to assign someone else to the case in two weeks. He gave me a choice. I can resign or be fired; either way I'm history. I think your job is safe."

"So you're giving up? Feeling sorry for yourself because you may have made a mistake? I say may have because we don't know for sure until we find Durant. In the meantime let's get DeMax back in jail, just in case. Get your ass back in gear and catch the son of a bitch, whoever he is. We've got two weeks."

Mecana looked at Darcie, placed his arms around her and gently drew her to him. "How can I refuse, Counselor?" he said as he held her.

"You better not," Darcie said.

He let go and leaned back in the seat. "Well, if we're going to do this let's start by talking to a friend of DeMax's. He may tell us where he is if we lean on him a little. Name's Tyrone Simmons. They call him Little T. Ran across him when me and Rustin Kemp was checking DeMax out."

"Some friend," Darcie said.

"Survival, my dear. Uno, number one. Called saving your own ass."

"I'm right behind you, Sherlock, lead on." She held her hands up over her face like she was expecting a blow.

Mecana smiled. "You are something special, lady."

"That's what I've been trying to tell you."

62

Tyrone Simmons' last known address was a rundown apartment building not far from DeMax. The tenants were mostly addicts that peddled drugs. Tyrone was one of them.

The front door was open to a filthy foyer with graffiti all over the door and walls. Two skinny black men with bloodshot eyes and needle marks all over their arms were sitting on the stairs. One looked to be in his forties, the other just out of his teens.

"You two lost?" the older one asked.

"No. You seen Little T?"

"What you want to know for?" the young one said.

"We're cops. He's not under arrest. But we need to talk to him."

"No shit. Surprise, surprise, ain't seen him," the older one said.

"He's around somewhere," the young one said.

"Shut up," the older one said.

"We'll find him," Mecana said and they stepped around the two men and started up the stairs.

In the next instant a small, thin black man with a shaved head, wearing a dirty white t-shirt and ragged jeans came flying down the stairs and knocked Darcie down as he pushed past her toward the front door.

"That's him!" Mecana yelled. "Stay put, I'll get him."

Darcie was struggling to her feet when Tyrone and Mecana disappeared out the front door. She ran to the door and saw Mecana chasing Tyrone down the street. The frail young man was no match for Mecana, who caught up with him at the end of the block and shoved him to the pavement. "I'm a cop! Stay down. Put your hands on your head."

"I know who you are. Seen you enough on TV."

Mecana cuffed him and got him to his feet. Darcie came running up.

"Think you broke my arm," he said, grimacing as he rubbed his arm.

"You shouldn't have run. We're not here to arrest you. We want to know were DeMax is," Mecana said.

"Ain't seen 'em. In jail last I heard."

"Out on bail but we need to find him. Thought you would know," Mecana said.

"Ain't his keeper, how would I know, man?"

"Not even if it meant going back to jail?"

"Heard about the women. DeMax like women too much to hurt 'em. Got the wrong nigger, man."

"If we don't find him someone else will, and they may kill him," Darcie said. "You don't want that."

"Lady, won't do no good to drop that stuff on me. Ain't seen 'em."

"If you don't want to talk, lean against the wall and spread 'em, Tyrone," Mecana said. "Let's see if you've got something in your pockets we can bust you for."

"Okay, I get it. He came by, gave me a few bucks and split. Didn't say where he was going."

"Is there a place you think he would go?" Darcie asked.

"Got a half-sister, don't know where she stays."

"That's a new one on me," Mecana said. "Mother or father?"

"Hell man, we don't know who our own daddy is. Maybe the same bastard. I'm his half-brother too."

"What's her name?" Darcie asked.

"Was Tameka Brown, two years ago."

"Anything else?" Mecana said.

"Don't know no mo'."

"Okay, Tyrone, you can go. Get yourself in rehab," Mecana said and took the cuffs off.

Tyrone didn't say anything, just rubbed his arm and was gone. Mecana and Darcie went back to the truck. The two black guys they ran into on the stairs were studying the chrome wheels on Mecana's truck.

"How would you guys like to visit our jail?" Mecana asked.

"What we do?" the old guy said.

"It's not what you did, but what you were thinking about doing, and if we hadn't showed up when we did, you would have done it," Darcie said.

The young one looked at the older guy with a confused look. "What the hell she say, Beagle?"

"Damn if I know, Bobby."

"Think about it. We saved you from committing a crime," Darcie said.

Mecana smiled and climbed in the truck. "Do you know who Yogi Berra is, Darcie?"

"Sure, why?"

Mecana paused, started to speak, and thought better of it. He gave Darcie a sideways look. "Never mind," he said and started the Silverado.

63

Mecana turned on his computer and ran Tameka Brown through the database. Twenty-one names came up, four blacks in Dallas, about DeMax's age.

The first three on the list didn't work out, but the fourth one's address was an old rundown apartment building not too far from where they had found Little T. It was obvious Little T was not completely truthful. With some questioning, they found her in one of the rooms with three other women.

She admitted she was DeMax's half sister. She was in her late-twenties but looked fifty. They had the same mother who died two years ago. She said she would tell them where he was for fifty dollars.

"How about for nothing," Mecana said, "before I book you for harboring a fugitive."

"Ain't here, left, don't know where he went," she said. "Just funnin' you." Her eyes were foggy from the drugs and her mind kind of came and went as she talked. She paused and went into a trance for a few seconds then came back. "There a reward for him?"

"No, other than you won't have to go to jail."

"What would I go to jail for? Didn't do nothin'."

"If you know where DeMax is and don't tell us you have. Now where is he?" Mecana asked.

She looked at Mecana with a blank stare again and batted her eyes. "Don't know." Mecana and Darcie could see it was useless talking to her anymore and left her sitting in a chair, staring at a wall.

They were getting back in the truck when DeMax came roaring up on his Harley, spotted them and took off.

Mecana spun the truck around and gave chase. DeMax cut the bike through a yard and came out on another street, the Silverado right behind him.

Mecana dodged some trashcans and bounced into the street. DeMax let the hammer down and was pulling away.

"He's headed for the freeway," Mecana said. "Call for backup."

Darcie picked up the mic. "Officer needs assistance, any unit. In pursuit of murder suspect on a Harley Davidson, Texas license number 136HFC. Headed north on Frugal 1600 Block. Intercept, may be armed."

DeMax hit the freeway doing ninety and begin weaving in and out of traffic. Three black and whites showed up in hot pursuit. DeMax jumped his Harley over a curb, made a turn off an exit into a residential neighborhood. A small boy on a bicycle appeared out of nowhere right in front of the Harley. DeMax swerved to miss him, lost control and the bike fell on its side and skidded down the street, chewing up DeMax's leg on the pavement as it went; finally coming to a stop some fifty feet later, still running.

The three units surrounded the bike, the officers got out with their weapons drawn. Mecana pulled up in the Silverado, siren going, lights flashing. He and Darcie jumped out of the truck.

"Cut the bike off, DeMax, it's over," Mecana said. De-Max reached up and turned off the ignition. "Don't move, DeMax. I'm going to get you up. You know the routine. Keep your hands on your head."

"Ain't got no gun," DeMax said. "Didn't want to go back to jail."

"Well, you played hell then because that's where you're going," Mecana said.

"My leg's broke," DeMax cried out.

"Call an ambulance, Darcie." Darcie nodded and dialed 911.

Mecana lifted the bike and DeMax slid his leg out from under it. His pants leg was torn off; his leg bloody. "Man, it's fucked up," he said. His face was showing the pain.

DeMax held his arms up and Mecana cuffed him. "We've got an ambulance coming, DeMax. Before anyone else gets here I want to ask you, did you kill Nadine or any of those other women?"

"Man, I didn't kill nobody," he said. "Somebody's settin' me up."

"Wish I could believe that," Mecana said.

"Fact, man, swear. Ain't killed nobody."

"We'll get you to a hospital, DeMax," Mecana said.

Darcie walked over to the officers. "Thanks, guys," she said. "We've got him now."

64

Mecana and Darcie put DeMax in the hospital for a broken leg with around the clock guards, and stopped off to file their reports.

Nick Booker walked in. He didn't look like a happy camper.

"I should punch you in the nose, Mecana. Just on general principal," Booker said.

"What's your problem, Nick?" Darcie asked.

"You need to find you a new partner, Darcie," Booker said. "Mecana's a bad influence on you."

"Booker, I don't know what your problem is," Mecana said, "but I'm going to solve it for you in about two seconds."

"Tough guy. That's what's turning you on. That right Darcie, tough talk. I bet that's all you are, Mecana."

"Nick, you've always have been a poor judge of people," Darcie said. "He will stomp a mud hole in your ass. Now calm down and tell us what this is all about."

"You talk me into getting bail for Baker and he murders someone as soon as he gets out of jail!"

"We're not sure of that," Mecana said.

"You made me a laughing stock!"

"So that's what this is about," Darcie said. "Your ego."

"I didn't do it for Baker. I did it for you, Darcie."

"Then you shouldn't be practicing law," Mecana said.

"Don't you know I still love you, Darcie?" Booker said.

"Me and about ten others," Darcie replied. "Go back to your office, Nick. I'll get DeMax another lawyer."

"If you want to leave here upright, Booker, you need to do it now," Mecana said. "DeMax is back in jail. You're off the hook."

"You know it wasn't all my fault, Darcie," Booker said. "You're a hard woman to live with." He noticed everyone staring at him, realized he had an audience and charged out the door.

Verves was standing in the doorway of his office, his coffee cup in hand. "Thought I was going to have to put you in jail for a minute there, Mecana," he said. "A lot of macho mojo going on. You're supposed to be able to control your emotions."

"Hey, I'm on borrowed time anyway. What the hell," Mecana said.

"Maybe less than you think. Finish that report for me, I have a briefing I have to go to," Verves said and walked away.

Darcie walked up to Mecana and put her hand on his shoulder. "Would you have really kicked his ass?" she asked.

"Just as sure as god made little green apples."

"I don't know what got into him. I haven't given him any reason to think I wanted to get back together. The meeting we had about DeMax is the first time I have talked to him in over a year."

"I think he was a little juiced, he'll get over it," Mecana said.

65

After the incident with Booker, Mecana and Darcie spent the afternoon checking Durant's computers without finding anything they didn't already know. Several of the other detectives came by to give their advice, none of which helped.

"Looks like we wasted an afternoon, Darcie," Mecana said. "You ready to call it a day? I'll take you home."

"Okay, tell you what, Mecana, I'm feeling domestic. If you want a free dinner, take me by the grocery store and I'll pick up whatever is your favorite and cook dinner for you."

"You have an ulterior motive, lady."

"No, thought I owed you one for you having to put up with Nick's behavior."

"You don't owe me anything, Darcie."

"Nevertheless, I would like to fix you dinner."

"Alright, I never turn down a free meal. Let's go."

After Darcie did her grocery shopping, Mecana drove her home and parked the Silverado in her driveway next to the Charger.

Each picked up a sack and made their way into the house. As they entered, they heard a noise in another room. Mecana drew his Glock.

"What the hell are you doing, Mecana?" Darcie asked.

"Someone's in the house," he said.

"My sister is here, flew in this morning. Put the gun away!"

"Sorry, a little jumpy," he said.

"Sis, I'm home!" Darcie yelled as they carried the groceries to the kitchen.

"I thought we we're going to have a really big meal for two with all the stuff you bought. Why didn't you tell me?" Mecana said.

"Slipped my mind."

Mecana and Darcie sat the groceries down and Darcie's sister walked into the kitchen.

"Hi," she said.

Mecana's mouth flew open. "My god there's two of you!" he exclaimed.

Darcie and Marcie both laughed.

"Mecana, this is my sister Marcie; we're twins."

"You sure are," Mecana said. "I'm Thomas Mecana, Darcie's partner. Everybody calls me Mecana."

"Glad to meet you, Mecana. Darcie has told me all about you."

"Well, she hasn't told me about you. She said she had a sister, but she didn't say anything about you being twins.

You look just alike, even your hair is the same style. I'm blown away."

"Why don't you and Marcie get acquainted, Mecana, and I'll fix dinner," Darcie said.

Mecana and Marcie went to the living room to talk and Darcie prepared dinner.

"Darcie tells me you're a teacher," Mecana said.

"Yes, although I'm thinking about getting into law enforcement like Darcie. Came up to have a talk with her about it. Thought we might open up a private detective agency together at one time, but she seems to be happy here since she became your partner," Marcie said.

"The feelings mutual. She's a good cop," Mecana said. "Tell you one thing, though, if you two worked together you would confuse the hell out of the bad guys. You could be in two places at once."

Marcie laughed. "Yes, everyone is always getting us mixed up."

"I may be leaving the department," Mecana said. "Maybe the three of us should have a talk about opening an agency."

"Anytime, if it's okay with Darcie," Marcie smiled.

"Married, Marcie?" Mecana asked.

"No, still looking. Darcie said you were divorced," Marcie said.

"Got two great kids, though," he replied.

Darcie sat the table with T-bone steaks, vegetables and a salad. Before they could cut the first piece of meat someone was banging on the front door.

"Who could that be, Darcie?" Mecana asked.

"I don't know. I'm not expecting anyone else."

Mecana got up and walked to the door and looked out the peephole. Nick Booker was standing there, his hair rumpled, one half of his shirt collar turned up; a wild look in his eyes.

Mecana opened the door. "What are you doing here, Booker?"

"Might ask you the same thing, buddy," Booker said, leaning against the side of the door. "You screwing my ex-wife?"

Darcie ran to the door. "Get the hell away from here, Nick! Don't you think you have already made a big enough fool of yourself?"

"I knew you were fucking this moron," Booker said, pointing a shaking hand at Mecana.

"My sister is here, we were having dinner, but it's not any of your business who I'm going to bed with!"

"Booker, go home before I have to put your ass in jail," Mecana said.

"You and what Army, asshole?" Booker said and swung at Mecana. Mecana ducked and caught him with a right cross. He fell backwards out of the open door, off the porch into the front yard. He didn't get up.

Darcie ran out the door and fell to her knees, looking at Booker. "Mecana, I think you killed him!"

Marcie came to the door. "Is he dead?" she asked.

Mecana walked over to Booker and looked down at him. "He'll come around in a minute. I just cold-cocked him. He'll be alright." Mecana bent down and slapped him a couple of times. Booker moaned and opened his eyes. "See, I told you."

"We can't leave him here," Darcie said. "Help me get him in your truck, we'll take him home."

"I'm not putting him in my truck. You still got a thing for him or something?"

"No, I just don't want to take him to jail. He would be disbarred."

Booker rose up on his elbows, shaking his head. "What the hell happened, where am I?"

"Call him a taxi," Mecana said. "I lost my appetite, I'm going home."

"Alright, go. You would do the same thing if it was your ex-wife," Darcie said.

"No, I wouldn't. The guy's on something, you want to get arrested, too?"

"Go home, Mecana, I'll handle it," Darcie said.

Mecana looked off into space, bent down and put his hands on his knees, looking at Booker. "Ah, shit. Let's put him in the truck."

"Can I help?" Marcie asked.

"No, I'll get him," Mecana said. "Darcie, you drive his car and lead the way to his house."

"Thanks, Mecana, I knew you would understand," she said.

"I don't understand, but I can't leave you here with him."

"I'll be alright. Marcie is spending the night."

"I'd feel better if I was spending the night, too."

"You can sleep on the couch."

Mecana smiled. "Figured that."

"Thanks," Darcie said placing her hand on Mecana's. "I really appreciate your help."

"I see now why Darcie speaks so highly of you, Mecana," Marcie said.

"Get in the car, Marcie," Darcie said and nudged her towards the car.

66

The next day Mecana and Darcie didn't talk about Booker, but there were some unsaid words that needed to be said. Finally, Darcie cleared the air.

"Mecana, thanks for helping me last night. I don't think we'll have any more trouble out of him. He called this morning, apologizing, said he was moving out of town."

"That's good. I put up with his shit for you, but I'm not sure whose side you're on."

"I'm on yours," she said. "Always have been."

Mecana looked at Darcie; she held eye contact with him to validate her comment.

"Okay, let's get back to chasing the bad guys and forget Booker," Mecana said.

"I'll never mention his name again," she said.

Mecana nodded and smiled. "You still owe me a steak dinner, lady."

Mecana and Darcie were on the street headed for the Silverado when a van came by with a big sign on the side, advertising a vacation in Costa Rica.

Darcie glanced at the sign and stopped. "Mecana, that advertisement on the van reminded me of something. There was a big travel-type poster in the guest house at the Durant's with Costa Rica on it. I didn't think anything about it at the time, but why would it be there if there was not some reason? What if that's where he went?"

"A long shot, but we don't have anything else," Mecana said and made a call to DFW airport security to check for him. It didn't take long for a computer check to confirm there was Flight 1245 from New York to Costa Rica on the day Durant's car turned up at the airport, and the flight did make a stop in Dallas.

Mecana whipped the Silverado up to the curb, flipped the flashing lights switch and walked away, leaving the truck sitting in a no parking area next to the entrance of the American Airlines counter.

Mecana and Darcie walked up to the counter and approached an attractive young female attendant. Mecana showed the attendant his badge.

"Miss, we're working a homicide and would appreciate your help"

"What do you need?" she asked.

"Would you check to see if a Doctor Dawson Durant boarded Flight 1245 from New York to Costa Rica on the 26th, for a departure of 1:35 P.M.? We ran a check before but they didn't turn up anything, may have missed this one."

Mecana took a pen from his pocket, wrote the numbers down, and handed her the paper.

"This will take a few minutes," she said and typed the information into her computer.

"Thank you," Mecana said. "We'll wait." Mecana turned to Darcie. "Maybe we will get lucky."

"He had to have a passport," Darcie said. "If he's on that flight they won't extradite him back if we're seeking the death penalty. They've had a law since 1877 against capital punishment. The only way we can get him back is if he comes back voluntarily, which isn't likely, or we waive the death penalty, and it would still be difficult. They're not too willing to extradite anyone unless they have already been convicted, which may be why he went there, if he did."

"How do you know all that?" Mecana asked.

"Just smart, I guess."

"Sure, level with me."

"A case I worked on."

"Sir," the attendant said, and stepped in front of Mecana to get his attention. "That name does not appear on the manifest. Seven passengers boarded the flight in Dallas. Here's the list." She handed it to Mecana.

He looked at the list. Three U.S. citizens, two female, and four native Costa Rican men. No Doctor Dawson Durant. "No Durant, but we've gone this far, let's check out the ones that did get on the flight," Mecana said.

"Customs could tell us," Darcie said. "They had to have passports to get out of the country and customs would have their records."

"Alright, you're the one that knows all this stuff. Lead on, my dear. Let's have a look."

"Start looking for a customs sign," Darcie said.

67

Mecana and Darcie walked up to a door with a 'U.S. Customs' seal on it and entered. A uniformed customs agent, a little overweight with puffy checks, was sitting at a desk behind a counter on the phone. Darcie took a seat and Mecana leaned on the counter and waited for the agent to get off the phone. Mecana visually surveyed the office. Various pictures of supervisors and the President hung on the walls. He could see the customs line through a big glass window on the other side of the office. People running their things through the x-ray.

The pudgy agent hung up the phone and got up and walked over to Mecana. "What can I do for you?" he asked.

"Dallas Police," Mecana said, and showed him the badge. "We have reason to believe that a passenger or passengers on a flight to Costa Rica yesterday may have been involved in a crime. We have the names and thought you could tell us about the status of their visas: addresses, etc."

"Do you have a warrant for their arrest? I need a warrant."

"No you don't," Darcie said. "We have probable cause that a crime has been committed and when we verify fingerprints we should have what we need to make an arrest for at least Grand Theft Auto. As a law agency, we need your help in doing that. That's called due process. Now, run the names please."

The agent leaned on the counter and looked at Mecana. "Is she for real?" he asked.

"I'm afraid so. She's a lawyer."

"I hope she's right," he said. "Give me the names." He took the list from Mecana and sat down at his computer and inserted the information and waited. A few minutes later the names popped up. He printed them out and handed them to Mecana. Darcie joined Mecana at the counter and they began to scan the list. All of them had thirty-day temporary visas except one. He had an indefinite work visa. The one with the work visa jumped out at them the minute they saw it: Rubio Dominguez. His employer - Lamont Estates. Occupation - Gardner.

"Look at that," Mecana said.

"Yes I see it," Darcie said.

"Thanks for your help, sir," Mecana said.

"No problem. I think. Good luck," he said and watched Mecana and Darcie leave.

Mecana called the lab and checked on the fingerprints from the car.

"Got some back," the tech said. "The doctor's, of course, the Sadler girl, and some we sent off to the FBI we don't have back. That's it."

"You're going to come up with a Sam Little. He's okay but the one I need to know about is a Rubio Dominguez. He worked for the Durants. I need to know as soon as possible. Especially if they were on the steering wheel or gearshift.

Call Washington and ask them to put a rush on it. He's on a work permit from Costa Rica. His prints should be on file from his passport. Call me," Mecana said and hung up.

"Okay," Mecana said to Darcie. "We may be able to break this log jam if Dominguez's prints are on the driver's side. He either stole it, or Lisa Durant knows more about her husband's disappearance than she's letting on."

"What if she says she was just helping him get to the airport and would pick up the car later?" Darcie asked.

"Durant didn't let anyone drive that car if he was around."

"I get you," Darcie said. "Why would she let him leave it at the airport if her husband was going to need it?"

"Exactly," Mecana said.

In less than an hour the tech called back. "It's his prints on the wheel, gearshift and dash. No criminal record, just the passport," he said.

"Thanks, that's what I needed. Lisa Durant has some explaining to do, Darcie."

"I would think so."

"It's looking more and more like one Doctor Durant is history," Mecana said, "and Lisa knows what happened to him. She's so damn smart, she hasn't left one trace of DNA or anything to help us find Durant. Maybe if I face her down she will slip up."

"Going to try the whore routine again?" Darcie said, staring at Mecana.

"Not on your life. Learned my lesson," Mecana said and shook his head.

PART SIX

68

Across town, another kind of meeting was taking place.

Robert Verves looked at the door with 'Quinton C. - Bolden Police Chief' on it, opened it, walked in, said hello to the Police Chief's secretary and sat down.

"Chief Bolden will see you in a few minutes, he's on the phone," she said.

Verves nodded. He looked at the coffee pot and thought about getting coffee, then changed his mind; he was too nervous. He knew what the Chief wanted to talk to him about - why Mecana was still on the job.

The secretary heard the phone drop back on the hook.

"You can go in now, Chief Verves," she said.

Verves got up and walked into the office.

The Police Chief was a husky man with thin red hair and deep blue eyes. He had a body like a middle linebacker, and no sense of humor.

"Have a seat, Robert, and tell me why Mecana is still out there."

"I gave him to the first of the month to resign or be fired. I thought we owed him that much after fifteen years."

"Normally, I would not have an objection to that, but the Mayor, District Attorney and a multitude of reporters are making my life miserable. They want this guy caught and Mecana's not doing it. Before you say anything, I know someone else will probably not do any better, but making a change will show we're trying to do something."

"Are you saying I should call him in and fire him now?" Verves asked.

"Yes, I want him gone immediately. You've got until tomorrow at quitting time to get his resignation, or fire him. I would prefer his resignation, looks better for us and it will give him more benefits."

"Then you're going to have to do it, Chief. I gave him my word," Verves said.

"Robert, sometimes you really puzzle me. You're a top cop with all the tools. I was going to recommend you for this job when I left, but if you can't take orders I don't know. I don't have anything personal against Mecana, it's just business; a part of being the boss. Sometimes you have to do what you don't want to do."

"There's something going on with the Durants and Mecana has got a handle on it. Let's give him a few more days anyway," Verves said.

"Mecana has blinders on, Robert. He's not exploring any other suspects and Durant has good alibis. I've looked over all the files and I don't find anything that would make him a suspect."

"Maybe not," Verves said. "But I've learned he has a nose for finding the truth. He has a reason to think Durant did it."

The Police Chief dropped his head and rubbed his forehead. "Robert, I have a problem with changing my orders. It doesn't look good to the other supervisors when I do it for one and not the other, but I'm going to make an exception. Today's Wednesday. I want his resignation on my desk by nine o'clock next Wednesday morning," he said.

"Okay, I can do that."

"If you don't, I want yours," the Chief said.

"Is that all, Chief?"

"Yes. Remember, no later than Wednesday morning, nine o'clock."

Verves nodded, got up and walked out.

69

Lisa Durant's Lexus wasn't parked in the driveway when Mecana brought the Silverado to a sudden stop and got out. The garage door was open; a sky-blue Silver Shadow Rolls Royce was the only car in the garage.

"Looks like we missed her," Darcie said.

"I'll see if her maid knows where she is," Mecana banged on the door several times with the knocker but no one came to the door. He walked back to the Silverado and cranked it. "Cover your ears, Darcie," he said and flipped two switches. Lights started flashing in the grill of the truck, rear lights going on and off, the siren screaming a shrill, ear-piercing sound.

The front door flew open and a frightened little woman, eyes as big as saucers, stood there looking at Mecana, not knowing whether to shit or go blind. Mecana saw her at the door, shaking, and cut the siren off.

"You know where Lisa Durant is?" he asked, walking towards her.

The frightened woman's words were stuck in her throat. She shook her head up and down trying to coax them out. Finally, the words jumped out. "Don't know. Go away."

"You sure you don't know where she is? You want me to turn that noise on again?"

"No, no, lady doing pictures."

"Where?"

"She say windmill where everybody goes. Don't know where."

"Windmill? What kind of windmill."

"Old place, shoot pictures. Don't know.

"You know Rubio Dominguez?"

"Uncle," she said. "Go back to Costa Rica."

"Why did he go back?"

"No more job. She buy him ticket, go home. I go soon."

"Did she tell him to drive Durant's car to the airport?"

"Don't know."

"Has Mr. Durant been home?"

"No. Lady say he gone away."

"Where?"

"She don't say."

Mecana nodded and walked back to his truck and got in.

"Well?" Darcie asked.

"Rubio Dominguez is her uncle. I think Lisa sent Dominguez to the airport in the car to get rid of it because she knew her husband wasn't going to be driving it anymore and it would look like he left in it. She didn't expect it to be found so soon. Durant's disappearance may be revenge for his infidelities."

"Or maybe worse," Darcie said. "She got even with her rivals for his affection, too. Only one catch: the surgery."

"Thought about that. Don't think that would be a problem with her. She may be a psycho, but a hundred-and-sixty-plus IQ gives her an advantage most killers don't have. She has all the medical books she needs at her disposal. She grew up in that atmosphere. A little practice and she'd be as good as any surgeon. If I was a betting man, I would bet the farm she got the drugs from her father, either as a patient or she discovered them and decided it was the way to a perfect crime. So far she's right. Her maid said she was shooting pictures at an old windmill where everybody goes. That ring a bell with you?"

"No, unless she's referring to the Old West Museum. There's a big windmill there," Darcie said.

"Let's go have a look."

When Mecana drove up, two men were setting up lights and a model was having oil applied to her body in preparation for the session. Lisa Durant was checking her cameras.

Mecana ran the Silverado up behind the Lexus, blocked her escape and got out.

Lisa walked up to the Silverado and put her hands on her hips.

"What now? You find Dawson?"

"You know we didn't, but I bet you did," Mecana said.

"What's that supposed to mean?"

"It means we think you murdered your husband, and five women," Darcie said.

"You know those kind of statements are grounds for a lawsuit," she said.

"Big on this lawsuit thing aren't you?" Mecana said.

"You've lost your mind, Mecana."

"You let the gardener drive your husband's car to the airport?" Mecana said. "He wouldn't let anyone drive that car, plus you were trying to get rid of it by hiding it in the airport."

"You came to that brilliant conclusion all by yourself because someone drove Dawson's car to the airport?" she asked. "I wasn't there, remember? How could I give him permission to drive the car? I gave you too much credit, Mecana. You're dumber than I thought."

"Unfortunately, you're right. I was after the wrong Durant. You're a horse of a different color."

"Spare me your hayseed analogies, Mecana."

"Were not done, lady. You're a clever woman, but not enough to get away with murder. You'll slip up and I'll come for you."

"Not in this lifetime," she said, her eyes narrowing with a faint smile. "If you had any evidence you wouldn't be standing there running your mouth. You better have that truck out of my way when I finish or I'll run it over."

"We'll be back," Mecana said.

She slung the camera straps over her shoulder and walked away. Mecana and Darcie got back in the truck and drove away.

"If we can get her for his murder, they can juice her for that," Mecana said. "But we don't have enough evidence to get a warrant on her. I may have to go back and take another look in that house, anyway."

"That's breaking and entering. You'd go to jail," Darcie said.

"At this point does it matter?"

"It does to me," Darcie said, rolling her eyes.

Mecana looked into those big brown eyes. "You ever find you a place to live?" he asked.

"No, not yet."

"Why don't you move in with me? It's just me rattling around in that big house, plenty of room. We could split the expenses. You could have your own bedroom and I wouldn't charge you any rent."

"What would you charge me?" she smiled.

"Whatever you wanted to pay," Mecana said and smiled, too.

"I'll think about it," she said. She leaned over and gently kissed him. "That was sweet. You're a good man, Thomas Mecana."

"Not according to Lisa Durant and Robert Verves," he said.

70

Mecana didn't tell Darcie he was going to his house.

"What are we doing here, Mecana? I thought we were going to plan our attack on Lisa Durant?"

"We are, but I thought I would give you the guided tour to help you decide what you wanted to do."

"I've seen it," she said.

"Kind of, mostly from a horizontal angle."

"That's not what you're thinking now, is it?" she asked.

"Nope." Mecana unlocked the door and he and Darcie walked in the house. "You can have the master bedroom if you like. I moved to the guest room when my ex-wife decided to leave."

"Why are you still living in a place that has so many memories?" Darcie asked.

"I guess that's just the reason. Makes missing my kids a little easier. They know where I am and this was where we had a lot of good times, as well as bad."

"You sure this is a good idea? Sounds like you're not ready for someone else in this house."

"No, it's alright. You're welcome to move in and do exactly what you want, except bring another man here. I don't think I could handle that."

"Then what you're really saying is you want me to be your partner and girlfriend?"

"Yeah, I guess you could say that. I'm not proposing marriage but I'm very fond of you, plus we make a good team."

"I don't know, I like my independence. Give me a little more time to think about it."

"Sure, take your time. Either way it's okay with me," he said. There wasn't any Jim Beam left but he had an expensive bottle of red wine he had been saving for a special occasion. And since he hadn't thought of one before today, he decided Darcie's visit would do.

"They tell me I make a mean spaghetti dinner, if you're interested. I got some good wine, too. It's about supper time."

"You cook, Mecana?" Darcie asked. "That doesn't sound right."

"There's a lot of things you don't know about me. If you move in you'll find out. I don't know if that's good or bad," he said and laughed. "You want dinner?"

"You sound serious. You apparently think you can cook. Why not, I'll live dangerously. Rattle those pots and pans. I'll get comfortable, as they say. That is, if I can borrow your bathroom."

"Help yourself. I'll start dinner."

Mecana started cooking dinner and a little later Darcie came in wearing Mecana's Marine shirt and sweat pants, carrying her clothes. "Which way to the washing machine?"

Mecana pointed at the door and she proceeded toward it. Her 38C bra fell to the floor and Mecana's eyes brightened as he gave the bra a curious look.

"Men," she said, shook her head, picked up the bra and continued to the utility room.

When she returned, Mecana had set the table. "Be ready in about ten minutes," he said.

"Tell me officer, are you trying to bribe me?"

"Crossed my mind, but I was too hungry."

"That's what I thought." She saw some pictures sitting on a dresser. "Tell me about your family," she said, pointing at the pictures.

"Well, that's my dad, my brother Ethan and me in the first one. My dad retired from the Marines, moved to Florida. I don't get to see him as much as I would like, and my brother is a career Marine officer. I tried to follow the family line but I didn't have a war, got bored with all the training and got out. That's my mom next to us, Melinda. She died of cancer ten years ago. She was a very special lady. I miss her very much. The other two pictures are my kids. Emily, who's grown into a beautiful young woman, and Morgan, who's not far behind."

"Quite a family," Darcie said.

"Thanks. Dinner's ready, let's eat," Mecana said.

Mecana fixed Darcie's plate and poured the wine.

"Hey, this is good," she said. "You can cook."

"Told you."

"It will be a while 'til my clothes get dry. Think I'll try out that bed you were telling me about after dinner."

Mecana nodded. "The bed's made. Tomorrow we'll take a drive down to Houston and have a talk with Lisa's father.

He may have left something out when he was questioned by the Houston Police. We need more background on her."

"Okay, thanks for the great dinner."

"You're welcome."

"You need some help with the dishes?" she asked.

"No, I've got it."

"You're definitely earning points," she said, and gave him a peck on the cheek.

"Take your time. I know it's a big decision."

71

It didn't take 20/20 vision to see that Doctor Lamont was the favorite of the rich. The women, even the old ones, looked like they were going to a fashion show, and the men to the bank.

Mecana walked up to the receptionist. She looked to be in her fifties, with bottle red hair, small eyes and mouth, too much makeup and several large diamond rings on her fingers. She looked at Mecana and Darcie; they didn't meet the dress code. "Do you have an appointment, sir?" she asked in a sarcastic tone.

"My name's Mecana, we're detectives from Dallas. We need a few minutes with the doctor. It's about his daughter."

Mecana could see he got her attention. Her chest began to rise and fall. "Has something happened to Lisa?" she asked and stood up.

"Something might, if we don't talk to him. We won't take long."

"Have a seat, I'll let him know."

"That's alright, we'll stand," Mecana said, as the lady opened the office door.

"You think bravado will do it?" Darcie asked.

"We'll see."

The receptionist came out of the doctor's office, held the door open and motioned for Mecana and Darcie to enter.

The first thing you saw when you walked in was a huge painting of Lisa. The office had big tinted windows, expensive furniture and a wet bar. A tall elderly gentleman, with perfect silver hair, green eyes and a stylish goatee, wearing an expensive gray suit, was helping himself to a drink. He didn't offer Mecana or Darcie one.

"You've got ten minutes to tell me what this is about, and it better be worth my time," he said.

"I think you will find it interesting," Mecana said, showing the doctor his badge.

"I know who you are from the news. You have been harassing my daughter and son-in-law unmercifully. But I also understand you will be gone in two weeks, otherwise I would have you in court by now."

"You do have your contacts, don't you," Darcie said.

"That I do, lady. Now what is so important that you thought you had to drive to Houston to see me? Make it quick, I've got a busy schedule."

"Alright," Mecana said. "Has your daughter ever been treated for any kind of mental disorder?"

"Did you find anything in her medical records? I know you had access to them."

"No," Darcie said.

"Then why ask me?"

"Did you treat her?" Mecana asked.

"What the hell are you getting at? What's your point?"

"Our point is we think your daughter is unbalanced," Mecana said.

"You're the one with the problem, Mecana. I see now why my daughter is so frightened of you."

"She told you that," Mecana said.

"Yes, you're making her physically ill. She's letting the servants go in preparation for closing up the house and moving back to Houston."

"Doctor, your daughter isn't afraid of the devil himself. She's playing games with you. Has your daughter ever been prescribed Ludimocson or been exposed to it in any way?"

"The drug was taken off the market years ago," Lamont said.

"We know, answer my question."

"I'm not going to answer anything," he said.

"You just did, Doctor. I know my place, and I know I'm not as smart as you and your daughter. But sometimes smart people can be pretty dumb. I didn't just fall off the turnip truck. Good day."

"Yeah, Doctor, what he said. Goodbye," Darcie said.

They came out of the office and the receptionist was standing by the door. The way she reacted she gave the impression she was more than a receptionist. Possibly the doctor's girlfriend.

She turned her nose up and walked back to her desk.

"You could have come in," Mecana said. "The secrets are the doctor's, not ours."

72

Mecana cruised up Interstate 45 toward Dallas, contemplating his next move.

"Well, we didn't get anything we can use in court, but I think we know where the drug came from," Darcie said.

"Only the police and the killer knew about the Ludimocson, but I bet Doctor Lamont knows now. I'm convinced he used the drug on Lisa, and she learned what it would do if you abused it."

"We still don't have any proof, other than the car incident, and that's not going to get us very far if we don't find Durant," Darcie said.

"Not only that but we're running out of time, as the doctor pointed out," Mecana added. "We have the entire country looking for Durant and he's nowhere to be found. Everything hinges on finding the Doctor. I think we have to think outside the box as they say. What would a genius like Lisa

Durant do with a body? I would think the unexpected, the last thing we would think she would do."

"Alright, what?" Darcie asked.

"I don't know, I'm thinking out loud. Maybe keep it in the house."

"Well, while you have your brain in gear you might also consider he may be very much alive and a part of the whole thing."

"That's true, but I don't think so. She's too much of a control freak," Mecana said.

"We have to get in that house again, one way or the other."

"Take me home. Let's sleep on it, maybe we will figure it out by tomorrow," Darcie said.

Mecana dropped Darcie off, stopped by the gym for a two-hour workout, picked up a salad and went home. No messages from his kids. He couldn't get his mind off the case.

73

He dressed and drove out to the mansion. Lisa's Lexus wasn't there. He sat some three blocks away, watching with his binoculars, and wondered how he was going to get back in. He knew the place was wired, and if he was caught breaking and entering Verves would throw the book at him. Only a few lights were on in the downstairs rooms. Her father said she was letting the staff go. Who was there? She may be gone for days, hours or minutes. Mecana's phone rang. It was Rustin. "Hello, Rustin?"

"Mecana, that thing I've been trying to remember came to me. Right before I was stabbed, I got a big whiff of a woman's perfume. The killer is a woman, Mecana, not a man."

"That does make a difference, doesn't it?" Mecana said.

"Yes, damn it! I wish I could have thought of it before now."

"Thanks, Rustin, I'll let you know what I find."

"Yeah, it isn't Doctor Durant after all," Rustin said.

"No, it isn't."

"Thought that would help."

"It sure does, thanks. Talk to you later." No sense raining on his parade, Mecana thought.

He cut his phone off and decided to take a closer look. He walked in the shadows to the mansion, peeked through the iron gate and didn't see anyone. No wires running on the fence. He grabbed the top of the six-foot stone fence and pulled himself up on top and jumped down on the other side. He ran to the mansion and hid in some shrubs. A few seconds later, car lights hit the driveway and he ducked down. The car pulled up to the gate and the gates opened. The car drove through and the gates closed. It was Lisa. She parked in the driveway, got out carrying a large Big Top Pizza. The Lexus was loaded with travel bags. All kinds of thoughts were going through Mecana's mind. Somehow he couldn't visualize rich people eating pizza, especially Lisa, or having an affair with DeMax.

She unlocked the door and carried the pizza inside. As she cleared the entrance, Mecana darted to the door and stuck a credit card in the doorway and it stopped the door from closing completely. He waited a few minutes and pushed the door slightly open. When he didn't see or hear anything he opened the door, left the card in the door and went in. All the furniture was covered with sheets. She was getting ready to move out. He carefully made his way down a hall, past the spiral staircase into another hallway. As he turned the doorknob to enter a room, he heard a noise and turned to look.

Lisa Durant was standing there with an automatic pointed at him, wearing Jeans and a white shirt with her hair tied back in a pony tail. That was the first time he had seen her in what he would call 'common folks' clothes.

"Want some pizza?" she said.

"No thanks," Mecana said, eyeing the automatic.

"Hand me the Glock, butt first," she said.

Mecana did as he was told and handed her the gun. She stuck it in her belt.

"Now what?" he asked.

"You're going to love this," she smiled. "I dismissed all the staff, was going back to Houston tonight until I figured out how to deal with you, and here you are to make it easy. First, I think I'll cut off your balls, eat pizza, and watch you die a little bit at a time. I expect you to put on a good show. Dawson did. He begged me not to do it, even pledged his undying love, but that's exactly what he got."

"What if I decide to get it over with and make a play for the gun? You shoot me, I'm done for and you don't get to have your fun."

"I'll cut them off anyway, but I warn you, I'm an excellent shot. You won't die immediately, and it will give me more pleasure."

"I believe you. In that case, you can count on a good show. I won't disappoint you."

"This way," she motioned the gun toward a bookshelf.

She walked to the shelf with Mecana in the lead and removed a book titled, "Jack the Ripper."

A plunger popped out of the wall and the shelf turned to allow room to walk through into another room.

"That's appropriate," Mecana said. "You're certainly the female version."

"You don't know the half of it. Go in."

They walked through the opening into a large room with the smell of formaldehyde. The old brick had been whitewashed. A large surgical light positioned on a stand hung over a steel operating table with metal clamps for the hands and feet. Next to the operating table was an instrument table. Except for an old rusted metal door at the far end of the room, it had the appearance of a hospital operating room with some extras. A folded plastic suit lay on a table, next to a row of five sealed-glass boxes filled with fluid containing the remains of the vagina of each of her victims. The boxes were labeled with their names. An un-posed photograph of the victims, that Lisa apparently took, hung above each box. At the end of the boxes was a large jar labeled 'Dawson Durant - A Cheater.' His testicles floating inside the jar. A phone-booth-sized glass box contained what was left of Doctor Dawson Durant. He was naked. His eyes were nothing but white round balls. His mouth gaped open, with blood bubbles floating around in the tank. His testicles were gone, his penis shriveled up so much it was almost sunk into his body.

"How do you like my little sanctuary, Mecana?"

"You are a very sick woman," Mecana said.

"I would like to think of myself as unique, different in my own way. Not like that do-goodie sister of mine. She tried to take the affection that was due me, so I pushed her off the roof. I think Daddy knew. I discovered later the drug Daddy gave me was what I needed, but for a different purpose. None of my friends were really friends. They hung out with me for the money. And Dawson, I made him what he was and he couldn't keep his dick in his pants. I had to have my revenge. You can understand that, can't you, Mecana?"

"No, not like this," Mecana replied.

"Got them all," she said. "Took the one thing they were most proud of, their sexuality. They paid the ultimate price."

"That's sure as hell an understatement. Does anyone else know about this?"

"No. It's my great-grandpa Jackson Bernard Lamont's and my little secret. I accidentally found the room when I removed a book and there it was. I put the Jack the Ripper book there later, kind of a tribute to my grandpa. There's more behind that door," she said, looking at the rusted metal door. "That's where grandpa kept his sex slaves and the corpses of people who got in his way. His missing wife is chained to the wall in there. There's much more but I don't feel like talking about it anymore. Let's get back to the matter at hand. Climb up on that table, Mecana."

Mecana changed the subject. "You do the surgeries?" he asked.

"Of course, nothing to it. I read up on it and found a couple of female bodies to practice on. Although that first slut of Dawson's was a little touch-and-go, with that nosey cop showing up. Enough talk, Mecana, take your pants off and get on the table."

He knew if she ever got him on the table he was done for.

"I don't think so. If you want me on that table you're going to have to kill me. No way I'm volunteering to have my nuts cut off."

"Alright, have it your way, but I'm not going to kill you right away. I want to see you suffer for the trouble you have caused me. How about I take your balls off with a bullet?"

"You're a real monster."

"Thank you. My grandpa would be proud," she said, and aimed the automatic at Mecana's crouch.

In the next instant, Darcie was standing in the doorway, her Beretta pointed at Lisa. Lisa glanced at Darcie, and hesitated. Darcie fired. A bullet hit Lisa in the chest. She staggered back against the wall.

"Bitch!" she said, struggling to raise the automatic. Mecana grabbed the Glock from her belt, pressed the barrel between her eyes and pulled the trigger, her emerald green eyes blinked and she made a slight jerk of her head, then dropped the automatic and slid down Mecana's body to the floor. Blood running through her long blonde hair onto the floor.

"You alright?" Darcie asked.

"How did you know I was here?"

"Thought you might be here when you didn't answer your phone. Saw your truck down the street. You men have a special relationship with your transportation. Knew you wouldn't be too far from that truck. Climbed up on the top of my car and jumped over the fence, walked in with out a problem."

"I didn't know you were that athletic."

"Was captain of my high school basketball team," she said.

"Lisa finally made a mistake," Mecana said. "Left the bookshelf door open, otherwise you would have never known I was here."

"You were wrong, it wasn't Doctor Durant."

"I was half right. We got backup coming?"

"Nope. I didn't have time to call. Why didn't you? You know your supposed to call for backup. That's what you're always telling me."

"I know. Everything happened so quick. I can understand why Rustin didn't call now."

"What is this place?" Darcie asked, looking around the room.

"Where a beautiful monster lived," Mecana said.

"My god. I'm going to be sick." She bent over, put her head in her hands and threw up.

"Good thing Doc Seymour's not here to see that, he would be bitching about you contaminating the crime scene again."

"To hell with Seymour. You two may have ice water in your veins, but I don't."

"Sorry I pissed you off."

"Me too," she said.

"Lisa said there was more in that room," Mecana said, pointing to the rusted metal door.

"You look, Mecana. I'm going to sit this one out."

Mecana holstered his Glock and pulled on the door. It made a screeching sound and stuck. He pulled on it again and it came open enough that he could see it was dark inside. The smell was worse than the formaldehyde. He felt a light switch inside the door and flipped the switch. A Light came on. He looked inside. A single bulb was suspended by a wire from the ceiling.

"Wait to call until I come back," Mecana said. She nodded.

Mecana slipped through the crack and slowly moved into the room. It was dirty and sweaty, with mildew fungus growing on the walls. Several large rats ran in between the old worn brick and disappeared.

About ten feet in he saw what Lisa told him about. A skeleton chained to the wall. From the size and pelvis he knew it was female. Bones were scattered all around, he recognized some of them as being human. Hand and foot shackles were mounted on the wall next to the skeleton.

An old tattered table with deep cut marks in the top was pushed up against the wall, and what looked like an eighteenth-century black weather-cracked leather Gladstone bag sitting on it. The bag was slightly open. He pushed the top back. Underneath a load of rat droppings he saw a sharpened rusted railroad spike, with what looked like bloodstains on it. What was left of a pink handkerchief was laying next to the railroad spike with 'S.H. Austin Symphony Member' on it. A small rusted ball-peen hammer and two long steel-bladed stained knifes. In the other compartment, a small leather purse with two shillings in it and the name 'Mary Jane Kelly' engraved inside the flap. 'J.G. Beard Leather Shop – London, July 1888' was stamped in the leather inside next to the letters 'JBL.'

"Darcie, come in here!" he yelled.

A voice came back "No, come out of there."

"You have to see this."

"Oh shit," bounced around the room. She came through the crack. "What is it? I've got to get out of here. One minute you're pissed off because I don't call in, then you're telling me not to."

"Alright we'll go, but look at this. You remember me telling you about Lisa's great-grandpa that built this place?"

"Yes. He owned a railroad, right?"

"Yes, and he was in Austin when those women that William Sidney Porter, better known as O. Henry, the short story writer, called the Servant Girl Annihilator murderers.

"The what murders?"

"Several women, and a couple of men, were murdered and mutilated, some survived, from New Years Eve 1884 to Christmas Eve 1885 in Austin. They called them the Annihilator Murders. The murderer drove a railroad spike through their ear into their brain with a hammer and cut off body parts.

"A railroad spike?"

"Yes, see the connection? And he was in London when Jack the Ripper murdered those women in 1888. This bag proves he did both. His tools are in the bag along with some souvenirs he kept."

"Come on, are you telling me Lisa's grandpa was Jack the Ripper?"

"That's why he was never caught. He left Austin and they gave up the chase for the killer shortly afterwards. He goes to London, does the same thing, then comes back to Texas. Only this time he builds his horror house in Dallas and continues his mayhem until he dies an old man, without anyone except his great-granddaughter ever figuring out who the hell he was."

"And grandpa's genes caught up with his great-granddaughter and turned her into a monster, too," Darcie said.

"Exactly," Mecana said.

"If it wasn't for the horrible things she did you could almost feel sorry for her," Darcie said.

"Almost," Mecana agreed.

"Do we try to prove you're right? We could make a lot of money."

"Maybe."

"Do I detect some hesitation in your voice?"

"Yes, it occurred to me we would never see another peaceful day the rest of our lives. The press and curiosity seekers would hound us forever about one thing or the other. If we leave the bag here they're going to come to the same conclusion and we would still be in the crosshairs."

"Are you thinking what I think you're thinking? You know we could wind up in jail." "Not if we just take the bag. The rest would be speculative. Nothing for sure and we get rid of the bag. We know who the Ripper was, but no one else ever will. We solved the most famous crime of all."

"We would be the only ones who know who Jack the Ripper really was."

"That's right, Sherlock," Mecana said, grinning. "If you agree, I'll get the bag."

"You're awful trusting. How do you know I won't change my mind?"

"Alright, then. Do you, Darcie Connors, promise to never reveal what we found here today, so help you god?"

Darcie put her hands on her hips and gave Mecana a cold stare. "Get the damn bag, Mecana. I'll make the call for the crime scene gang."

"You're sure?" Mecana said.

"Yes, I agree. Our life would be hell. Not to mention the souvenir hunters that would tear this place down brick by brick and dig up the old man. That's something I don't want to be a part of."

Mecana took the bag to his truck and hid it in his tool box. By the time he got back to the mansion, the police and ambulances were arriving.

74

The expression on everyone's faces defied description as they wandered through the carnage, looking at something they found very hard to believe.

Mecana and Darcie by now just felt numb.

Verves arrived and stared at the boxes, mesmerized for several minutes without saying a word.

The medics put Lisa in a body bag and were collecting the vagina boxes. No one seemed to know what to do with Dawson Durant. Doctor Seymour decided they would re-move him from the box. Poor bastard, all because he liked women too much.

The press had gotten wind of what was going on by some big mouth cop and were coming to the scene by the dozens.

Verves leaned up against the wall, his knees weak. He finally found his voice. "Unbelievable. How the hell did you find this, Mecana?"

"I would like to tell you through my shrewd detective work. But the truth is, as a last resort, I came to the mansion looking for I-didn't-know-what. Then Lisa showed up. Darcie saved my ass and I whacked Lisa when I got the chance."

"Well, you were on the right trail," Verve said. "Forget the letter. No way am I going to let you resign. Come by in the morning and we'll talk about your next assignment. I have to go deal with the press now. You want to help me?"

"I don't think so, Chief. Not exactly my cup of tea."

Verves frowned, took a deep breath, rolled his tongue around in his mouth like he had a bad taste in it. "How do you describe or explain something like this? It's so inhumane. It's like a nightmare you can't wake up from."

"Lisa didn't think so," Mecana said. "She thought she was getting even for being betrayed and that they deserved what they got."

"Sick woman. Maybe too smart," Verves said.

"Maybe so," Mecana said.

"I think you and Darcie are due a commendation for valor. See you in the morning." Verves left to face the media mob.

Darcie was listening, and walked over to Mecana. "My, how the worm has turned," she said to Mecana. "Yesterday he couldn't wait to get rid of you, now you're his fair-haired boy."

"It's kind of disgusting, isn't it?" Mecana said.

"Right now, I think you could run for Mayor and beat Pratt."

75

A large crowd of reporters and spectators had gathered outside police headquarters, waiting for Mecana and Darcie to arrive. Someone had spilled the beans and they knew they were coming.

He parked the Silverado at a parking meter across the street and got out, took a taped-up cardboard box out of the truck tool box and put it under his arm.

"What's that?" Darcie asked, puzzled.

Mecana turned the box so she could see the writing on it. It read 'POLICE PROPERTY - CASE 16385. FILE UNTIL NEEDED.'

"You're kidding," Darcie said.

"No, it may be there forever. No one's going to call for something they don't know about. But if it is ever found, I say I took it to the property room and forgot to tell them."

"Mecana, you may have come close to losing them, but you do have balls. You're going to just walk through the crowd with that box under your arm?"

"Yep," he said.

"What the hell, lets do it," Darcie said and smiled.

The reporters rushed them as they crossed the street, almost knocking the box out of Mecana's hand. The red headed TV reporter looked at the box. "What's in there, Mecana?" she asked, the camera focusing in on the box.

"Evidence," Mecana said.

"Can we see it?"

"No, sorry."

Someone yelled from the back of the crowd, "You going to give us a statement?"

"After I meet with Chief Verves, I'll talk to you."

"What about you, Miss Connors?" the TV reporter asked.

"It's over, time to move on," she said and Mecana nodded in agreement.

"That's it?" the reporter asked.

"That's it," Darcie said and glanced at Mecana.

Mecana smiled and tightened his grip on the cardboard box.

A young, athletic-looking man with a notepad and pen stepped in front of Mecana. "What are you going to do next, Mecana?"

"That's up to the department," Mecana said. "Let us through, please."

"What about you, Miss Connors?" the young man asked.

"I'm with him. Whatever they tell us to do," Darcie replied.

Mecana dropped the box off in the property room, and he and Darcie took the elevator up to Chief Verve's office.

76

Mecana and Darcie were surprised to see the Police Chief, Mayor and District Attorney there. They all began to applaud. Chief Verves was the first to reach them. He shook hands with Mecana and hugged Darcie.

"Mecana, thanks to you and Darcie, the case is closed," Verves said. "We found Cindy Freeman's house key in that horror chamber, along with personal items from the other victims.

"That's what Lisa was looking for in the office," Darcie said. "The keys to Nadine's apartment. That's why she left the key in the door; it was a message for me, for catching her snooping around in the office."

"Lisa said she practiced on two bodies," Mecana said. "It probably happened in Houston."

"We may never know," Verves said. "But there is something I know you will like. The FBI transferred Sullivan and his partner to Los Angles." Verves patted Mecana and Darcie on the back and laughed.

Mecana looked around the room at all the people that wanted his head yesterday but were praising him today. They all looked away when he made eye contact with them.

The Mayor walked over and stuck out his hand for Mecana to shake. Mecana looked at it and turned away.

"What are you doing, Mecana?" Verves asked, embarrassed. "Let bygones be bygones. It's over. Everyone is here to show their appreciation."

"That's right," the District Attorney said. "We don't hold a grudge. You shouldn't. It all worked out okay."

"That's right," Police Chief Bolden echoed.

"What about DeMax?" Mecana said.

"We dropped the charges this morning, he's a free man," the District Attorney said.

"Let's celebrate, Mecana," Verves said.

"Thanks, but no thanks, Chief. You're all a bunch of damn hypocrites." He took off his badge and Glock and dropped them on a nearby table before walking away.

Everyone was stunned in silence, including Darcie. She looked at the badge and gun on the table, studying them for a moment. She sat her Coke down, removed her Beretta and badge from her purse and laid them on the table beside Mecana's.

"Wait up, Mecana." She followed him out of the room. "You've got to help me move."

THE END

About the Author

John L. Lansdale was born and raised in East Texas. He is married to the love of his life Mary. They have four children. He is a retired Army reserve Psychological Operations Officer and a combat veteran with numerous medals and awards. Past roles include inventor, country music songwriter and performer, and television programmer. He produced and directed the Television Special "Ladies of Country Music." He has also produced several albums in Nashville, hosted his own radio shows and won awards for producing and writing radio and television commercials.

Lansdale was a writer and editor of a business newspaper. He has worked as a comic book writer for Tales from the Crypt, IDW, Grave Tales, Cemetery Dance and several more. He co-authored the Shadows West and Hell's Bounty novels with his brother Joe R. Lansdale. He is also the author of Zombie Gold, Horse of a Different Color, Slow Bullet, When the Night Bird Sings, Broken Moon, The Last Good Day, Long Walk Home and several more titles soon to be released.

<u>**THE MECANA SERIES by John L. Lansdale**</u>
#1 - Horse of a Different Color
#2 - When the Night Bird Sings
#3 - Twisted Justice

<u>**Titles by John L. Lansdale**</u>
Slow Bullet
Zombie Gold
The Last Good Day
Broken Moon
Shadows West (with Joe R. Lansdale)
Hell's Bounty (with Joe R. Lansdale)
Boy and Hog (Short Story)
Emergency Christmas (Short Story)
Tales from the Crypt (Comic Series)
That Hellbound Train (Graphic Novel)
Yours Truly, Jack the Ripper (Graphic Novel)
Shadow Warrior (Graphic Novel)
Justin Case (Graphic Novel)

SLOW BULLET
by John L. Lansdale

A "page-turner... Those who like their thrillers with
a heavy dose of violent action will be satisfied."
- *Publishers Weekly*

In this timely novel, Clark McKay, a retired Army Special
Forces Colonel, has developed a drinking problem after losing his
wife and son in a car accident, as well as from the nightmares of
his Vietnam days. And he's not getting any younger. In spite of
his problems, he is determined to find out who murdered his best
friend and his friend's wife.

A Washington D.C. detective refuses to believe McKay has
found the murderer, a former CIA operative and arms dealer who
murdered McKay's friend because he discovered the truth behind
the assassination of JFK – preventing President John F. Kennedy
from ending the Vietnam War.

McKay learns there are CIA documents his friend hid that
will prove the conspiracy to be true. His search for these
documents takes him all over the world. On his journey, after
wading through all the corruption, McKay is brought to the
conclusion that he may have to resort to murder if justice is to be
served.

What happened over fifty years ago is still with us today. In
fact, many still doubt the "lone gunman" theory put forth by the
Warren Commission. Could there truly have been a conspiracy to
keep JFK from ending the war?

Truth and fiction make an interesting mixture in this fast-
paced and entertaining novel. There are always those who escape
justice. One hand washes the other, unless you have someone like
Clark McKay who is willing to pay the ultimate price.

"Slow Bullet is a straight-ahead thriller...it's about
action, and there's plenty of that. Check it out."
– *Bill Crider's Pop Culture Magazine*

WHEN THE NIGHT BIRD SINGS
a Mecana Novella
by John L. Lansdale

Shortly after solving the horrific Mutilator serial killer case, Thomas Mecana and Darcie Connors are on the trail of a new suspect.

On the inaugural day of their own private investigation firm, the two detectives meet Candy Kane - a lascivious Dallas socialite who offers them a small fortune in exchange for protection.

A former patient of her psychotherapist husband has been trying to settle old scores by threatening Mrs. Kane' life.

And he's not the only one out for vengeance.

With an ever-growing suspect list, Mecana must toe the line between friend and foe.

Each action leaves them sitting in the crosshairs of those wanting to claim the Kane fortune.

One wrong move could mean the end.

"…the author's innate ability to spin a complex tale painted with vivid characters and intense suspense provides readers with a well-paced book that they may find difficult to set down."
– *Amazing Stories* review of **Horse of a Different Color**

TWISTED JUSTICE
a Mecana Novella
by John L. Lansdale

Newlywed private detectives Thomas Mecana and Darcie Connors have barely shaken their honeymoon jetlag before taking on another case in the Lone Star State.

Dallas Homicide Detective Sunday Verves is looking into the suspicious deaths of local drug runners when she discovers a potential suspect that hits too close to home – Angela, the daughter of her superior officer, and Angela's lawyer boyfriend.

When the trail leads her south of the border, Verves enlists her old friend Mecana and his new wife into tracking down Angela and her boyfriend.

What they discover down Mexico way turns the case on its head and sends the group searching for clues to a bigger piece of the puzzle.

Ultimately, Sunday Verves finds she must choose between avenging wrongs of the past or righting wrongs of the present.

Sometimes the only choice is TWISTED JUSTICE.

LONG WALK HOME
a novel by
John L. Lansdale

Ten-year-old Trenton O'Rourke's life was changed forever during the summer of 1944. He and his family lived on a fading farm like many others in the small town of Angel Point, Mississippi. With family members fighting in World War II overseas, and rising racial tensions back home, what was normally a routine summer turned into a nightmare of murder, loss, trying to cope with hard times to survive and surprise learning experiences of growing up. Trenton's life would have never been what it was had it not been for a chance encounter with someone nobody expected.

Keep your eyes peeled for

THE LAST GOOD DAY
by John L. Lansdale

and

BROKEN MOON
by John L. Lansdale

Two new Westerns from
John L. Lansdale and BookVoice Publishing

<u>Follow us online at</u>
www.bookvoicepublishing.com
www.twitter.com/mybookvoice
www.goodreads.com/johnllansdale
www.facebook.com/bookvoicepublishing

All Keiron wants is a quiet life. Fat chance with a boyfriend like Bren. But if he thought Bren complicated his life, that was nothing compared to the complications that begin when he opens the door to what he thinks is a naked boy claiming to be his slave.

Draven is a fairy with his sights set on the handsome human who keeps a wild place in the garden for fairies. When Draven slips through a fairy gate into the city, he sets in motion a series of events that binds him to Keiron forever, and just might be the end of him.

While Draven explores Keiron's world with wide-eyed wonder, Keiron does everything he can to keep Draven's at bay, until the only way to save Draven and bring him home is to step into a world that should exist only in children stories.

A NineStar Press Publication

Published by NineStar Press
P.O. Box 91792,
Albuquerque, New Mexico, 87199 USA.
www.ninestarpress.com

Fairies at the Bottom of the Garden

ISBN: 978-1-947904-23-1

Printed in the USA
First Edition
November, 2017

Also available in eBook

ISBN: 978-1-947904-22-4